Mr.L_____

S0-BOE-534

Mr. Lemke

Mystery
at
Bluff Point Dunes

MYSTERY

—at—

BLUFF POINT DUNES

Lisa Eisenberg

Dial Books for Young Readers

NEW YORK

Published by Dial Books for Young Readers
A Division of NAL Penguin Inc.
2 Park Avenue
New York, New York 10016

Published simultaneously in Canada
by Fitzhenry & Whiteside Limited, Toronto
Copyright © 1988 by Lisa Eisenberg
All rights reserved
Design adapted by Amy Berniker
Printed in the U.S.A.
First Edition
(a)
1 3 5 7 9 10 8 6 4 2

Library of Congress Cataloging in Publication Data

Eisenberg, Lisa.
Mystery at Bluff Point Dunes.

Summary: While visiting her friend's grandparents
on Cape Cod, Kate Clancy determines to find out who
has been stealing small objects from the house,
only to uncover a much more dangerous plot.
[1. Mystery and detective stories.]   I. Title.
PZ7.E345Ms 1988   [Fic]   87-24454
ISBN 0-8037-0527-1

To all the grandparents, past and present
L. E.

1

The airplane hit a patch of choppy air and rocked like
the Riptide Rollerama at Magic Mountain. My stomach
rocked right along with it, and then yowled out loud.
Once again I cursed myself for scarfing down all that
plastic airline food. It had seemed like a good idea at the
time. I'd been bored to tears, and scraping morsels of
lunch off the tiny doll-china dishes had been the only
fun around. It hadn't been easy, what with my elbows
hunched up against my ribs and the plane jouncing
around and everything, but I'd kept at it, and eventually
I'd managed to eat every bite.

Now I was paying the price for my pig-out. The frozen
roll, chicken Toledo, saffron-pimiento rice and Jell-O-

pineapple-cheesecake had congealed together into a giant bowling ball of a lump in the middle of my poor stomach. With every lurch of the plane, I clutched my airsickness bag more desperately. What am I doing on this crate anyway? I asked myself after one stunningly sickening swoop. Why am I, a home-loving Southern California fourteen-year-old, flying all the way across the country just to go to the beach?

I turned to stare at the person next to me, and I remembered the reason why: Bonnie Bennington, my friend from Pacifico High School in Los Angeles. Bonnie's grandparents, Eunice and Brewster Bennington, own a cottage right on the beach in a place called Bluff Point Dunes in Cape Cod, Massachusetts. Every summer Bonnie goes to stay with them for a month so she can bask in the sun, and they can dote on her and buy her things.

The arrangement sounded heavenly to me, but apparently Bonnie hadn't thought so. In fact according to her, she'd announced in June that she wasn't going to the Cape at all this summer. When her parents had pressed her for a reason, she'd refused to discuss the matter. This had caused her mother and father to express concern about their daughter's lack of family feeling, and a long, complicated process of delicate negotiation had followed. After weeks of discussion Bonnie and her parents had reached a compromise. Bonnie would go to Cape Cod if and only if: 1) She only had to stay for two weeks instead of a month, and 2) She could invite a friend along on the trip.

Bonnie had told me all this while we were running laps around the gym one day right before the beginning of vacation, and I'd been dumbfounded. "Negotiations!" I'd gasped with my tongue hanging out of my mouth. "Weeks of discussion! Compromises!" Those things are unheard of in my house. I mean, my mom and dad deal in ultimatums, and when they deliver "The Word," they're not exactly expecting to be met with a counter-proposal from me!

Yes, I'd been amazed at Bonnie's descriptions of her family's polite conferences around the dinner table. And I'd been even more amazed to learn that her parents had practically had to force normally easygoing Bonnie to go on such a fantastic vacation. But I'd been the most amazed when she'd told me that the person she wanted to take to Cape Cod was me, Kate Clancy!

It's not that Bonnie and I aren't friends, because we are. She seems to appreciate my sick sense of humor, and I know I appreciate her warm smile and her habit of looking on the bright side of things. We're thrown together all the time at school because our gym lockers are side by side, and we sit next to each other in the back of algebra where we swap elaborate notebook doodles. Sometimes we even eat lunch with the same crowd. But that's about as far as it goes. We never see each other after school, and I'm not even sure where Bonnie's house is. Anyone looking at the two of us would instantly realize that we come from different worlds—maybe even from different species! She's a ray of sunshine, and I'm a human rain cloud. She's beautiful, and I'm 'interesting.' She has millions of great clothes, and I have three boring outfits that I cleverly mix and match. She's really popular, and I'm—well I could go on and on but it's too painful, and you get the idea: Bonnie Bennington and I have just about as much in common as a chocolate soufflé and a pudding pop.

This moment was a perfect example of what I'm saying. My brown hair was frizzing out around my head like an electrified pom-pom. My Hawaiian shirt was all wrinkled, and my white shorts were bunched up and speckled with crumbs from my lunch roll. I didn't have a mirror with me, but given the condition of my stomach I could be pretty sure my 'interesting' face was pale and clammy.

Bonnie, on the other hand, looked like one of the models in the mail-order catalog she was reading. Her fair, chin-length hair sat on her head like a neat, shiny cap. Her expensive little Lacoste dress looked like it had just been pressed. Naturally Bonnie hadn't even considered eating the airline lunch, so she was totally crumb free. And unlike me she wasn't feeling as sick as a dog.

Unnngh. I leaned back in my seat again and tried to ignore my stomach. Instead I daydreamed about the days ahead of me. Just think, I told myself. Two whole weeks away from home. Two whole weeks at a quaint little beach cottage right on the ocean. Two whole weeks of sun, surf, and picnics on the sand . . . elegant Bennington picnics with watercress sandwiches, and pickled onions, and oily little smoked oysters . . . *mmmmmuuuunnnngh!*

This time my stomach was so loud I was sure the other passengers must have heard. Would this flight never end? I glanced down at my brand new plastic watch and saw that we only had about half an hour left till we landed in Boston. That made me feel a little better. Half an hour wasn't so long. Besides, looking at my new watch always cheered me up. I'd bought it with my own money especially for this trip, and it had taken me several days of hard shopping to find it. The strap was half red and half blue, and the dial was the Statue of Liberty's green face with great big shiny silver numbers on it. My father said it made him dizzy just to look at it.

Bonnie closed her catalog and put it away. "Excuse me, Kate," she said with a soft little swing of her perfectly-cut hair. "I'm afraid I have to get out to go to the ladies' room."

I couldn't believe it. Bonnie had been to the bathroom about four times in the last two hours, and here she was asking to go again. I unbuckled my seat belt and stood up so she could squeeze past me into the aisle.

Oh well, I told myself, Bonnie was probably running to the bathroom because she was nervous about something. Maybe for once she'd found something she couldn't "Think Positive" about. In fact now that I thought about it, she'd been jumpy and irritable during most of the flight. First she'd refused to eat any lunch. Then she'd complained about a crying baby and a bratty kid who was running up and down in the aisles. She'd said she loathed the movie, and the flight attendants' uniforms were tacky, and she hated having seats right over the wing.

That much griping might not be unusual for some people (me for instance), but it was extraordinary for Bonnie. She's one of those people who like to walk on the sunny side of the street. At school when the two of us are together, she's always the easygoing one, telling me that our gym teacher, Ms. Neurenberg, isn't really a vicious sadist, or that the green meat loaf in the cafeteria isn't really baked dog, and so forth. But so far on this trip Bonnie had been the opposite of her usual self. She'd been complaining about everything. And the closer we got to Boston, the more she was finding to moan about.

I suspected her bad mood had to do with seeing her grandparents and having me meet them and everything. As I said before, I already knew that Bonnie hadn't really wanted to visit them in the first place, so it wasn't hard to guess that they were odd in some way. This was certainly a feeling I could identify with. I'm mortified by every single member of my family, but particularly by my grandparents. It's not that I don't love them, because of course I do. But they are truly embarrassing to be seen in public with. If you don't believe me, remind me to tell you about the time my Grandpa Mike lit a match to read a menu in a dark restaurant and set fire to his napkin and Grandma Irene had to throw a pitcher of Diet Pepsi all over him to put it out.

Anyway, back to the present. Bonnie returned from the bathroom, and the pilot announced that he was beginning his descent into the Boston airport. We dutifully rebuckled our seat belts, put our dropdown tray tables into their original upright positions and checked to see that our carry-on luggage wasn't sticking out into the aisle.

"Do you have a lot of relatives in Cape Cod?" I asked Bonnie. "Are there any cousins our age?"

My friend jumped in her seat and stared at me as if I'd asked her to skydive out the emergency exit. My ears were stopped up from the change in altitude, so my voice may have been a bit loud, but still . . .

My face must have reflected some of my built-up annoyance because Bonnie looked at me in surprise and then gave herself a little shake. She treated me to one of her incredibly warm generous smiles, and I immediately felt one hundred percent happier. "I'm sorry, Kate," said my friend. "I guess I've been a pretty hopeless companion on this trip."

She was right. She'd been a king-sized pill. But I felt a rush of sympathy for her anyway. "That's okay, Bonnie."

She gazed out the window, and when she spoke again, it was almost as if she were talking to herself. "I just hope this trip works out okay. I hope we get to have some fun. But after the way it was last summer, I just don't know. . . ."

Her voice trailed off, and I knew that my theory about her grandparents had to be right. There was something appallingly weird about them. But what in the world could be that bad? If she only knew what *my* family could be like! The pilot aimed for the airport, and we hopped down onto the runway and taxied toward the terminal building. With my usual optimism, I'd been expecting a crash landing, so I was surprised and relieved at how smoothly the trip had gone so far. If I'd known what the future had in store for me, I might not have felt quite so carefree.

Clutching our carry-on luggage we staggered up and mashed ourselves out into the line of hot, sweaty passengers waiting in the center aisle of the plane. After what seemed like an eternity the line finally got moving and we made our way through the tunnel to the terminal. *NnnnnNNNNNrrrgh*. Oh, great. My stomach was having its usual reaction to the idea of meeting new people. With a long shuddering sigh, I tried to ignore my queasy insides and brace myself for my first encounter with Bonnie's eccentric old grandparents.

2

We came out into the waiting area, and I scanned the faces, trying to pick out Bonnie's grandparents. No one looked very likely. There was a slim youthful platinum-blond couple in tennis outfits, four sailors in uniform, and an exhausted man and woman with a baby and two little kids. The Benningtons must be late, I decided. Or else they'd forgotten to meet our plane.

You can imagine my surprise when the slim, youthful couple in tennis whites charged up to Bonnie and smothered her with kisses. At first I thought they must be some cousins my friend had forgotten to tell me about. But then I heard Bonnie calling them grandmama and grandpapa.

Could it be true? It was impossible to believe. But as I gaped at the man and woman, I realized they were older than I'd thought. Their platinum-blond hair was actually silvery white, and their slender well-bred faces were crisscrossed with fine little age lines. Still, they both had such fantastic tans and looked so smashing in their tennis outfits that they just couldn't be grandparents!

But they were. Bonnie introduced them to me as Eunice and Brewster Bennington, which I knew were her grandparents' names, so there was just no getting around it. At first I was too surprised and intimidated to speak. I mean, I'd been expecting a chubby, cozy old grandma and grandpa like my own, and instead I was face-to-face with a pair of aristocratic tennis pros!

Bonnie gave me a nudge with her elbow, but I still couldn't find my voice. Eunice must have noticed my discombobulation because she put a hand on my arm, gazed right into my eyes, and gave me a grandmotherly version of Bonnie's magnificent smile. Fortunately Eunice's smile also had the same warming effect on me, because all at once my voice came back, and I heard myself saying, "Hello" and "It's nice to meet you." Not exactly scintillating, but at least I was talking again.

Brewster asked me how the flight had been, but before I could answer, he'd picked up my overnight bag as if it weighed nothing (which, trust me, it didn't!) and headed off toward the baggage claim so briskly we had to run to keep up with him. Definitely the fastest grandfather east of the Rockies.

As we bounded through the terminal, Eunice asked if we were hungry, and Bonnie said she wasn't. I, on the other hand, realized that my stomach was back to its old form, telling me I was starving! We kept passing snack bars as we scurried along, and finally I suggested stopping for a hot dog and fries. Eunice started to laugh a refined laugh, as if she thought I'd been joking, but she stopped abruptly when she realized I'd been dead serious. "Oh, no, Kate dear," she said. (Actually she said, "Kate, de-ah," but I can't possibly imitate the Benningtons' cultured East Coast accents. If you've seen any old movies of President Kennedy, you'll have a good idea of how they sounded.) "Oh, no, Kate dear, Hettie will have high tea waiting for us at the cottage. She'll be terribly offended if you two famished young girls don't gobble up everything in sight when you arrive. Besides," she added tactfully, "I think it's just possible that the food here might make you dreadfully ill."

Well what could I say? I didn't know who Hettie was, or what high tea was either, so I couldn't exactly comment on that. I *did* know the hot dog and fries wouldn't make me sick (once I'm on solid ground, I can eat anything), but Eunice seemed so genuinely concerned for my health that I kept my mouth closed about that subject as well. Actually there wouldn't have been any time for a snack anyway. The three of us were practically running to catch up with Brewster as he sprinted through the crowd surging toward the down escalator.

We found our luggage with no problem, and before long everything was loaded into the Benningtons' old but distinguished Mercedes. Brewster got behind the wheel, and I soon discovered that he drove just the same way he walked—fast and crazy. What's worse, everyone in Boston seemed to drive the same way, charging in front of us from side streets, drag racing through stop signs, changing four lanes at a time without signaling. Once a driver honked at Brewster for failing to run a red light, so then of course Brewster *did*!

To make matters worse Brewster kept up a running Chamber-of-Commerce commentary as he drove, twisting his head around to talk to me, waving both hands at once and pointing out the window at the passing sights. The Hancock Building, the Prudential Tower, the Charles River, Harvard—you name it, he pointed it out. I really appreciated Brewster's enthusiasm for my education as a tourist, but by the time we were out of the greater metropolitan area, I was a nervous wreck. I turned to mutter something to Bonnie, but to my surprise I saw that she was completely engrossed in her conversation with her grandmother and oblivious to the danger we were in.

What's going on here? I asked myself. When we'd left the airplane, if you'd asked me if Bonnie was still in her jumpy mood, I'd have given you a definite "yes." She'd been fiddling with the clasp on her Gucci luggage and complaining about how crowded the airport was; I even thought I'd heard her mutter that she needed to go to the bathroom again! But then, miraculously, when she'd seen her grandparents, it was as if she just couldn't stay crabby anymore. I guess it made sense. After all, Bonnie is basically a naturally happy person, and the Benningtons had been so bouncy and jolly about seeing her, that in spite of herself she'd been infected by their good mood.

Now Bonnie and her grandmother were chattering away like best friends. Bonnie was telling stories about some of our warped classmates at school, and Eunice was laughing and exclaiming and saying, "Surely you must be joking!" As I listened, I felt a little jealous. I couldn't imagine having a grandmother who was not only thin and elegant but who actually thought my friends were amusing. Whenever I tell my grandparents about the kids I know, they automatically launch into their "Kids Today" speeches. (You know the routine: Kids today don't know the value of a dollar. Kids today never have to lift a finger. Kids today all have purple hair.) Anyway, Eunice seemed to be one grandmother in a million, and when I thought about it, I realized I was dumb to be jealous. I should be thrilled she'd been able to cheer Bonnie up. Who cares why Bonnie was so crabby on the plane? She's okay now, and that's what matters.

Still the whole thing was a puzzle, and there's one Velcro-like part of my brain that sticks onto a puzzle for dear life, no matter how hard I try to rip it loose. Now that I'd met the Benningtons I was even more mystified than before. The fact was that my airplane theory was dead wrong. Bonnie's grandparents were *not* embarrassing. Eunice and Brewster were a lot more presentable than most kids' *parents*, particularly my own. Why, I asked myself, had Bonnie tried to weasel out of visiting them this summer? Why had she been so irritable on the plane? Why had she said she wondered if we'd have any fun on this trip, after what had happened 'last summer'?

Thinking about these 'why' questions helped me not to think about some other 'why' questions, such as, why Brewster was driving so fast, and why the car was weaving back and forth across the center line as we sped toward our destination. Fortunately, once we got away from Boston, the oncoming traffic thinned out, and I was able to relax slightly and enjoy the scenery. The trip to Bluff Point was almost three hours long, and as we drove, Brewster continued eagerly pointing out every single sight along the way. We passed signs for a lot of places I'd heard of before, like Plymouth and Hyannis, and I felt a little thrill of excitement. Brewster seemed to know everything there was to know about the history, geography, and wildlife of Cape Cod, and in spite of my anxiety about his driving, I had to admit he was interesting. He was so fascinated by the place himself, he couldn't help communicating his enthusiasm.

"Cape Cod is shaped something like an unfinished backward *C*," he explained with a terrifying flourish of both hands. "Bluff Point Dunes, where the cottage is, is on the upper outside edge. To get there we have to drive about as far as one can go without actually plunging into the sea."

With Brewster at the wheel, plunging into the sea didn't seem all that farfetched, but naturally I didn't express this thought out loud. The closer we got to Bluff Point Dunes, the fewer houses, people, and traffic we saw, and Brewster explained that we were driving through the Cape Cod National Seashore, a protected area where no one was allowed to build anymore. "All this scraggly vegetation on the hillsides helps prevent erosion," he said. "Though those of us who live here have come to face our inevitable fates. Someday our beautiful dunes will all be washed away."

This statement made me look at the landscape with new eyes. Now the rolling, rugged dunes we were passing took on a kind of tragic, doomed quality. Finally, when the scenery began looking dramatically wild and wind-blown, we turned off the main road. Soon we turned again onto a little dirt road that led toward the east, and then we veered sharply onto another even littler dirt road that went up a steep little hill. The hearty Mercedes bounced to the top and slammed to a stop.

"Here we are, Kate dear!" Eunice trilled. "Bluff Point Dunes Cottage."

I didn't answer because, once again, I'd lost my voice.

As I gawked out the car window, my eyes bugged out of my head. Who were the Benningtons kidding? I mean, I know what a cottage is. It's someplace little and cute, like the witch's gingerbread house in *Hansel and Gretel* or maybe the hut where the three bears live. But the Benningtons' cottage wasn't like that. The Benningtons' cottage was an enormous mansion! True, it had been weathered by the sea air, and it was probably as old as the hills it was built on. But that only made it appear more elegant and graceful.

Mechanically I opened the car door and staggered out. I gazed up at the house and started counting windows, but lost track somewhere around seventeen. Then a loud, roaring noise caught my attention. I turned around and gasped with delight. The whole Atlantic Ocean was spread out below, glistening and inviting in the afternoon sun. The Bennington dune was one of the highest on the coast, and the view was gorgeous. Naturally enough the roaring noise turned out to be the waves, pounding on the sand at the base of the dune. A few yards away I saw a pretty little summer-house-type building, which I believe my mother would refer to as a gazebo. Just beyond the gazebo an incredibly long wooden staircase led right down the side of the dune to the beach.

If I'd been by myself, I would have kicked off my shoes and taken the stairs to the water. You may be wondering why I was so worked up about a beach, coming from L.A. and all, but what most people don't realize is that L.A. is a big place. My family lives a good twenty miles in from the coast, and going to the beach is always a major expedition in the station wagon with my father crabbing about the traffic and my mother fretting about overexposure to the sun. Now and then my friends and I go to the beach ourselves, but that means packing into a hot, disgusting, crowded bus that takes at least an hour and a half bouncing along on Wilshire Boulevard. So now do you understand what I was so excited about? I was staying in a place where the ocean was right in the back yard. In fact, the ocean *was* the back yard!

I could have stood and stared at the Atlantic all day, but Bonnie was pulling on my arm. "Come on inside, Kate," she said. "I want to show you our rooms."

The inside of the house turned out to be even less cottage-like than the outside. True, most of the furniture was aged white wicker or painted white wood, and the floors were worn old wooden planks covered with even older Persian rugs. But as I wandered from room to gigantic room, I saw several crystal chandeliers hanging from the ceilings and gold-framed paintings suspended from every wall. And mixed in with the light, summery wicker furniture were things like gleaming little wooden end tables, hand-carved Chinese chests, and delicate little porcelain clocks and figurines.

Bonnie danced ahead of me to the first floor, showing me the basketball stadium living room with a walk-in stone fireplace and the special children's dining room (honest!) off the main dining room. She skipped right by the wide, sweeping staircase in the front hall, and instead led the way up a narrow little set of stairs in the back of the giant country kitchen filled with a lot of lethal-looking, low hanging copper pots. On the second floor she took me to our rooms. They both faced the front of the house and were connected by a big old bathroom, which we'd be sharing.

When I opened the door to my room, I wanted to burst into song. It was awe-inspiring. It wasn't just the size, or the pretty painted furniture or the bright bedspread. It was the fantastic light. That special bleached-out ocean sunshine poured in through a pair of sparkling, million-paned windows and made little flickering gleams dance all over the pale yellow walls. I mean, I felt like Dorothy, suddenly transported right over the rainbow, somewhere in the middle of Oz.

When I turned to look at Bonnie, she was grinning and watching my face. "It's a terrific place, isn't it?" she said. "I knew you'd love it here."

"Then why didn't you . . . ?" I began. But my friend interrupted as if I hadn't even spoken. "I feel like a dirty dishrag," she said. "I'm going to wash up. Then we can go back downstairs and see what Hettie put out for tea."

I was still puzzled by my friend's major attitude change, but I was so in love with my wonderful room, I decided not to worry about it. As soon as Bonnie was gone, I hurried to the big windows to check out the view. To my total, absolute bliss, I saw that the windows weren't really windows at all, but doors opening out to my very own balcony overlooking the ocean. I was outside in an instant, gazing down at the pretty little gazebo I'd noticed from the driveway, listening to the surf and the seagulls and wishing I could stay in Bluff Point Dunes Cottage forever. It was a perfect place. How could Bonnie have even thought of not coming? She must be nuts! Maybe I could trade places with her. Maybe, I fantasized, Eunice and Brewster would learn to love me this week and decide to adopt me. That way I could come visit every summer for the rest of my life.

I took a big breath of sea air and leaned over the railing. From this angle I observed a kind of circular sandy path that seemed to go all around the outside of the house. I also saw that every room on this side of the cottage had its own ocean-view balcony, and that the corners of the balcony railings were decorated with big clay pots of red geranium plants. When I stood back up to look at my own flowers, I was disappointed to see that they were actually quite sickly. One of them wasn't blooming at all, and the leaves were turning ugly shades of yellow and brown. When I stuck my finger in the dirt in the pot, it came out completely dry.

I'm not much of a gardener, but the least I could do was give the poor plant a drink. "Get some water from the bathroom," I ordered myself. "As soon as Bonnie comes out." Just then I heard her make a noise in the room behind me. "Hey, Bon," I began, yelling over my shoulder. "Why didn't you tell me . . . ?"

As I spoke I turned away from the railing. Then I stopped cold. My friend wasn't behind me after all. Instead I saw a short, powerful, ugly little man with a patch over one eye. He was wearing faded blue overalls with grotesque, reddish brown stains all over the front. Spaghetti sauce? Or blood!

No time to figure it out. Because now the man was slowly moving toward me. And as he moved the sunlight glinted blindingly off the gigantic razor-sharp knife he was holding in his stubby, filthy right hand.

3

I gasped and stepped backward, smashing myself against the balcony railing, and praying that the weathered wood was stronger than it looked. The man in the stained overalls moved toward me, still clutching the oversized knife. His pitbull of a face contorted into an alarmingly ferocious expression, and low growling sounds came from the back of his throat. I tried to scream, but I couldn't.

In that split second I made up my mind. I'd jump. It was a long way down, but it was a better way to die than being hacked to bits by that knife. I grabbed the railing and started to turn around. But just then, behind the short man's back, the bathroom door opened and Bonnie sauntered into my room. "The sink's all yours, Kate," she said cheerfully. "Oh, hi, Waldo! I was just about to come downstairs to look for you and Hettie."

Breathless, I waited for my murderous intruder to whirl around and threaten Bonnie with his knife. Instead, to my absolute amazement, at the sound of my friend's voice the man's ugly features twisted, stretched, and scrunched up, all at the same time. At first I thought he might be having a fit—but then I realized he was smiling!

He turned around and faced Bonnie. "Welcome home, little Bonnet," he said. His voice was still more like a growl than a voice, but it certainly sounded a lot more human than the noises he'd been making a few minutes ago. "Hettie sent me up. The tea's gettin' cold. The other guests are startin' in already."

He shuffled to the door and left, and Bonnie finally noticed my halfway-over-the-railing position on the balcony. She blinked, frowned, and started to speak. But then she seemed to change her mind.

I took a wobbly step forward. "Who was *that*?" I asked. My voice was high and shaky.

"Oh, that's just Waldo. He and his wife, Hettie, have worked for Eunice and Brewster forever. I've known them all my life. They live in an apartment up on the third floor." Her voice was casual. *Too* casual, I thought.

"But . . . he just appeared in here, Bonnie! I turned around, and there he was. Before you came in, he was j-just about t-t-to . . ."

Bonnie didn't let me finish my sentence. "He probably knocked but you didn't hear him because of the surf." She came out on the balcony, and looked at me closely. "Gosh, Kate. You were really scared! I guess Waldo could appear a little unusual when you're not used to him. But he's really just a big puppy."

"Unusual!" I screeched. "Puppy!" This was taking looking on the sunny side to the point of frying your brain. "The man was waving a knife at me, Bonnie!"

Bonnie laughed. "Waldo is the gardener, Kate! That wasn't a knife, for heaven's sake. That was his scythe. He uses it to cut back the long grass by the driveway."

"Oh," I said in a small voice. "Oh." The blood rushed to my face. "He's the gardener. It wasn't a knife. It was a scythe." The grotesque, reddish brown stains had been dirt, fertilizer, and plant food. And I was a moron.

"Come on," Bonnie said. "Let's go downstairs and eat up the cucumber sandwiches before they're gone. I'm starving, aren't you?"

Well for once in my life I wasn't. I was still shaken and my appetite was completely gone. Also, Waldo had said something that was bothering me. "Bonnie, who are these other guests Waldo was talking about just now?"

"Other guests?" Bonnie looked puzzled. "I'm not sure . . . oh, he must mean the Kingsleys. But they're not really guests. That is, no one thinks of them that way. They're more like family really. They've been coming out here every July ever since I can remember. In fact they usually stay in this very room. It's a regular tradition."

Well tradition or not, I wished someone had told me there were going to be other guests in the house. In the first place I hate meeting new people and making small talk, and in the second place I felt and probably looked like a piece of ABC gum. As I gazed at Bonnie's neat little dress and clean little face, I realized I was even grubbier and more wrinkled than ever. I was in no condition to meet two more upperclass strangers.

"Go ahead without me, Bon," I said. "I'll take a quick shower and meet you downstairs."

"I'll save you some sandwiches and cake," she promised, with one of her quick smiles. When she was gone, I raced to my suitcase and began clawing through my stuff, desperately searching for something impressive enough to wear while sipping tea (which I hate) with a bunch of bluebloods.

After a long, frustrating paw-through, I finally settled on the new, fire-engine red dress I'd bought on Melrose Avenue especially for this trip. I loved it, even though my mom said it looked more like a baggy, oversized shirt than a dress. I had my doubts about wearing it on the first day of the visit since I'd only brought one other dress (what with all the bathing suits, there hadn't been much room in my suitcase), but I decided it was important to make a good first impression.

I also decided to wear my favorite piece of jewelry with it—the antique locket my cousin Monty sent me for my fourteenth birthday. It wasn't a family heirloom (our family doesn't have any), but it certainly looked like one, and it was one of the only classy things I owned. It was gold and heart-shaped, and I loved it.

I put the locket next to my Statue of Liberty watch on top of the white dresser. Then I peeled off my disgusting shorts and shirt, and headed for the bathroom. The shower in the big old claw-footed tub turned out to be hot, powerful, and soothing. As I lathered up with a big cake of lavender soap, I realized that my pulse rate was just now returning to normal after my experience with Waldo. You made a fool of yourself, Clancy, I said to myself. You overreacted like a total hysterical dope.

To my surprise, myself stubbornly refused to agree. *Did you really overreact?* it shot back through the steam. *Or is that just what Bonnie wants you to think? Isn't it more likely that Waldo was actually trying to scare you? Look at the facts: He sneaks into your room without knocking. . . .*

Wait! I said. Bonnie said he probably knocked but I didn't hear him because of the surf.

Get real! myself answered. *Since when are you supposed to go on into someone's room when they don't answer your knock? Anyway, as I was saying, Waldo sneaks into your room without knocking, he comes up behind you without saying anything, points a knife at you. . . .*

It was a scythe, I pointed out. He's the gardener.

Stop interrupting! Scythe or not, it's still sharp and deadly, and he didn't need to bring it in the house with him. If he was so innocent, why didn't he tell you about the tea instead of waiting till Bonnie came in?

Whew! I had to admit I'd made some good points. As usual, my inner voice was right. Waldo might not have been trying to kill me (I hoped), but he almost certainly had been trying to scare me. But why? Did it have something to do with whatever Bonnie had been worrying about on the plane? Had Waldo mistaken me for someone else? Or was the Benningtons' gardener hopelessly insane?

With this cheerful thought, I climbed out of the tub and reached for a towel. The one I found was soft, purple, and fluffy, and huge enough to wrap around myself twice. Luxury is wonderful, I thought as I dried off. I don't want there to be anything wrong with the cottage at Bluff Point Dunes. I want to have a perfect visit. I won't let myself be bothered with strange undercurrents or mysterious puzzles. As for Waldo . . . well, *whatever* his problem is, I'll just have to keep out of his way and hope he keeps out of mine.

I left the bathroom and started getting dressed. As I pulled my dress over my head, I became aware of a heavy flowery scent in the room. I didn't mind the smell, but I was puzzled because I was positive it hadn't been there before. I knew it couldn't be coming from the flowers on the balcony because they were half-dead, and geraniums don't give off much of an odor anyway.

Uh-oh. With a start, I thought of the lavender soap in the bathtub. I'd liked it so much, I'd lathered up at least three times. Though I hadn't noticed a heavy scent in the shower, the soap had to be the answer. I smelled like a perfume factory, but it was too late to do anything about it. I only hoped no one downstairs would notice.

I zipped up my dress and went to put on my watch and locket. I crossed the room to the white dresser where I'd left them. Then I blinked and did a double take. The top of the dresser was as white and empty as the top of a freshly licked scoop of vanilla ice cream. Both my new watch and my antique locket had vanished without a trace.

4

"You left the stuff someplace else, you absent-minded cretin!" I said out loud. "Stop being a panicky fool and look around the room!"

But even as I hurled these insults at myself, I knew I wasn't being fair. At home I probably would have deserved them. My room there is a mess, and there are millions of cluttered surfaces where two small pieces of jewelry might be hiding. But here there just hadn't been time to create my usual chaos. I hadn't put anything anywhere, so there was no place to look. Except for my dress, I hadn't unpacked at all.

I made myself go into the bathroom and poke around, even though I knew I never would have taken my jewelry in there. Then I came out and checked the top of the dresser again, as if the watch and locket might have miraculously rematerialized somehow. But of course they hadn't.

All at once I felt a surge of anger. What kind of house was this anyway? I step out on the balcony, and someone comes in and waves a knife at me. I step into the shower, and someone comes in and rips off my favorite watch and locket! Suddenly my beautiful sunny room seemed ugly and threatening; the light flickers taunting and sinister. I couldn't stand to be alone there one second longer. I pushed my toes into my favorite floppy sandals, and practically ran out the door and into the hallway.

With my shoes slapping up and down against the bottoms of my feet, I dashed down the narrow back stairway Bonnie had used on our way up. When I burst out into the kitchen, the first sight I saw was my pal, Waldo. He was drinking coffee at a large, scarred wooden table that looked like it doubled as a butcher block. As I went by him, he put down his cup and glowered at me with his one mean eye. Upstairs it had been clear to me that Waldo had a soft spot in his heart for Bonnie, or little Bonnet as he'd called her. Unfortunately, from the way he was looking at me now, it was painfully clear that the soft spot wasn't big enough to include little Bonnet's little friend.

I wanted to march up to Waldo and accuse him of stealing my watch and locket—but of course I didn't because I was scared to death of him, and I didn't have the slightest shred of evidence. Without saying a word I ducked under a rack of copper pots and hurried by the table in the direction of the dining room door. As I reached it, the door swung inward and a big, bony, haggard woman marched into the kitchen. She was carrying an empty tray, and I knew right away she had to be the famous Hettie everyone kept talking about.

She was as tall as her husband was short, and her expression was harried and put-upon. When she saw me, her eyes narrowed, and I had the sensation that she was just about to say something to me, but I'll never know whether it would have been pleasant or nasty. I probably should have stayed to hear her out, but I just didn't have the nerve. After what had happened upstairs, I wanted to put as many rooms as possible between me and Waldo. Without slowing down I caught the still-moving dining room door on its backward swing and kept right on going out of the kitchen. If Hettie wants to talk to me, I said to myself, she'll just have to wait until Waldo's been chained up for the night.

The dining room was empty, but I heard voices coming from the gargantuan living room. When I got there, I found Bonnie with Eunice and Brewster. All three of them were gracefully lounging on loveseats and munching teensy-weensy sandwiches with gross-looking curly green leaves sticking out of the sides. A big teapot and several trays of little cakes and more sandwiches sat on the glass coffee table. There was no sign of the other guests Waldo had mentioned.

I stood awkwardly in the doorway waiting for someone to notice me. I'd been planning to tell Bonnie about my locket and watch as soon as I saw her, but this formal little tea party didn't seem like the right time or place. I'd have to wait till I got her alone.

"There you are, Kate dear!" Eunice called to me. "I put my head in your room a few moments ago to check

27

on you, but I heard you in the shower. Do you have everything you need?"

Before I could answer, Brewster said, "Tea, Kate?" and grabbed up the big china pot from the table.

Yuck, I thought. But I didn't have time to think of a way to refuse, because Brewster was already bounding across the room and thrusting a tiny, delicate, steaming cup at me, and I was politely saying, "Thank you." As I spoke, I got another whiff of the heavy flowery scent from my room and wished I'd taken the time to get back in the shower and rinse off some of the lavender soap smell.

At that instant I realized someone was standing right behind me. Waldo again! I jumped and sloshed hot tea onto my fingers. But it wasn't Waldo after all. A total stranger was walking—or more accurately, *bouncing*—into the room, loudly apologizing for being late. "Terrifically sorry, all!" he boomed. "Hope you didn't wait tea on my account. Getting most terribly absentminded, don't you know. Such a grand house as this, it takes forever to find one's way downstairs. Not to mention the most vexing little problem upstairs. Held me up."

I turned to get a better view of the newcomer, and my chin just about hit my teacup. From his loud voice and choppy sentence-fragments, I'd been expecting some kind of English colonel type of person, maybe with a uniform and a cane. But this guy was truly funny-looking. He must have been about Eunice's and Brewster's age, but instead of being tall and slender, he was short and round as a donut hole. But that wasn't the amazing thing. The amazing thing was his huge handlebar mustache. It drooped way down on both sides of his mouth, and then suddenly jutted straight out sideways in front of his jowly red cheeks. Closer staring on my part revealed that the ends of the mustache were all stuck up with big globs of clear wax. The mustache was the same odd orangey brown color as the stranger's hair, which I'm pretty sure was a toupee.

"What little problem are you referring to, Theo?" Eunice asked the man. "How can I help?" As Theo started to answer, Eunice caught sight of me, standing awkwardly in the doorway, balancing my still-full teacup. She moved over to my side and put her arm across the back of my shoulders. "But before you tell us your troubles, Theo, let me introduce you to Kate Clancy, Bonnie's great chum from Los Angeles. Kate, this is Theo Kingsley, one of our oldest, dearest friends."

"Don't know about the dearest part, Eunie!" Theo said. "But I haven't a doubt about the oldest!" He roared at his own wit, and everyone else laughed politely. Except for me, that is. I couldn't bring myself to laugh at such a dumb joke, and besides, I was afraid I'd spill some more of my tea if I made the slightest movement. "Anyway, muh dear girl," the man said to me, "I'm very pleased to make your acquaintance. Eunie's put you in our regular room, don't you know. But we were happy to move out so you could be next door to your pal. And all the rooms at Bluff Point Dunes Cottage are beautiful, so we don't give a hoot where we're put."

Brewster passed Theo the tray of cakes, and he helped

himself to a goopy white one with pink frosting. "You were about to tell us about your vexing little problem," Eunice reminded him.

"Just misplaced my favorite abalone tie clip, is all," he responded. "Happened right after you stopped by to say hullo, Eunie. But don't go getting all bothered about it. Nothing fancy, no great loss. You know how it goes. Put something down someplace. Turn around for a minute. Turn back, the thing's vanished! Wasted half an hour searching for the blasted thing, then decided on my bow tie. But Mopsy won't give up. She's still up there, crawling around on the floorboards getting splinters in her knees!"

Theo roared with laughter again, but this time he roared all alone. Brewster was frowning and staring down at the pattern on the Persian rug. Eunice had become totally absorbed in pouring more tea—even though everyone already had a full cup. Bonnie had stopped chewing her sandwich in mid-bite and was sitting absolutely frozen on the couch, like some kind of blond-haired popsicle.

I, of course, was busily trying to figure out the implications of what I'd just heard and seen. Naturally I'd noticed that Theo's experience with his tie clip was almost exactly the same as my experience with my locket and watch. But I was more intrigued by the Benningtons' reactions—or non-reactions—to their friend's story. As of yet, they hadn't heard about my stuff vanishing, and as far as they knew, Theo had most likely dropped his tie clip down the bathroom drain the last time he was waxing his mustache. His "vexing little problem" shouldn't have been any big deal, but that's *not* how the Benningtons were acting. It was obvious that the news about the missing tie clip had thrown the three of them for a loop. But it was even more obvious that they were all trying to pretend everything was copacetic.

As I stared at the scene in the living room, my breath came faster, and my blood raced in my veins. My sixth sense detected a mystery in the air. It was unmistakable. I've had a few experiences with mysteries before, and I'm beginning to have a pretty good nose for them.

Here I go again, I told myself. I was half-excited, half-scared.

Oh, no you don't! myself answered. *This time you're going to keep your nose out of trouble! You're not going to get involved.*

But I already am involved! I responded. My stuff is missing too!

I'll never know what myself would have told me, because at that moment, yet another character floated onto the scene. A slightly dumpy woman in a flowing purple dress wandered down the steps and on into the living room. Her gray hair was pulled back into a wispy bun, and the expression in her watery blue eyes was both puzzled and apologetic. Now *this*, I told myself, is what a grandmother is supposed to look like.

"Hello, Mopsy, pet!" Theo said to the woman. "Find the tie clip?"

The puzzled look deepened. "Tie clip, Theo dear? I wasn't looking for your tie clip. Why, goodness me, I didn't even know it was missing. Why, I've been looking for *my* diamond bracelet."

"Well, did you find that then, pet?"

"No, sweetie, I'm afraid I didn't!" Mopsy gazed around the room without really focusing on anything. Finally she fixed her gaze on Eunice. "I'm very much afraid, dear Eunice, that our intruder from last summer has returned and made off with my bracelet. Shall you or I be the one to notify the authorities?"

5

If I'd thought Bonnie was frozen before, now she was positively glacial. Brewster had gotten to his feet and was pacing back and forth across the rug in his brisk way. All at once Eunice laughed out loud. "You can't be serious, Mopsy," she said. "There's no need to call in the authorities at this point. You know how we oldsters tend to misplace things. After tea I'll come up to your room with you and the two of us will give it a thorough going-over. I'm positive your bracelet—and Theo's tie clip— will turn out to be caught in a mattress, or stuck under a shoe, or hiding in some equally unlikely spot."

"But surely, Eunice dearest," Mopsy began, "after last summer—" Before she could say anything more, Theo shot a meaningful glance at Eunice, took a firm grip on his wife's arm, and led her over to a spot on a loveseat. "Eunie's perfectly right, pet," he said. His booming voice had become remarkably soothing and gentle. "We're just a pair of forgetful fogies who'd lose their heads if they weren't welded on. Come and have some tea, and then we'll send a search party upstairs to find our things."

With a vague little shrug, Mopsy allowed her husband to pour her a cup of tea and fix her a plate of little cakes and sandwiches. Her watery eyes still looked puzzled, though, and I was fairly certain she hadn't forgotten about her missing bracelet. Once or twice I caught her gazing over in my direction, undoubtedly wondering who I was and what I was doing there. I was still standing near the doorway, clutching my teacup, and mulling over the phrase "after last summer." Bonnie had used it on the plane, and now Mopsy had used it in the living room. But what were they talking about?

After Mopsy had eaten the sandwiches and cakes on her plate, she got to her feet and drifted over to me. "I don't believe we've been introduced," she said. Her accent was the same as Eunice's, but unlike Eunice's firm definite tones, Mopsy's voice was soft and whispery.

"I'm Kate Clancy," I said. I tried to make eye contact as I said this, but Mopsy seemed to be staring at something in the air, just to the left of my face. It made me a little nervous, but I kept on talking anyway. "I'm a friend of Bonnie's from California. We go to school together there."

Mrs. Kingsley smiled. Her smile wasn't as stunning

as Bonnie's or Eunice's, but it was pleasant and nice, and well, *grandmotherly*, somehow. "Of course, dear," she said. "You're the friend who's staying in our regular room. I'm so glad you're here to keep Bonnie company. You know, Eunice and I went to school together when we were girls. Oh my, that was a long time ago, wasn't it? She was the most beautiful girl, the rest of us always envied her so—in fact we still do, those of us that are still around and still have our wits." She giggled breathlessly at her little joke, and I found myself smiling too. "Yes, indeed, those were the golden days, my dear, when life wasn't so trying as it can be nowadays. Not that we're not having a wonderful time this summer as we always do on the Cape. Of course it used to be even more fun when we had our own dear cottage up the beach, but that became just too costly to hold onto and . . ."

The doorbell interrupted whatever it was Mopsy had been planning to tell me about her former cottage. Out in the hall I heard stomping footsteps—probably Hettie's—going to the front door, which opened and closed with two loud complaining *crrreaks*. A few seconds later a boy and girl about my age came into the living room. "Hi, Grandma," the boy said. "Hi, Gramps! Hi, Bonnie! When did you get here?"

I was pretty confused about who these kids were until Eunice broke off a conversation she'd been having with Theo, exclaimed with delight, and practically ran across the room to hug and kiss both of them. I decided they must be some local cousins Bonnie had never gotten

34

around to telling me about. While Eunice was hugging the boy, I couldn't help staring at him. Before I had a chance to look away, he spotted me over his grandmother's shoulder. For a brief, excruciating instant our eyes locked, and it hit me that I was gawking like a lovesick puppy dog, waiting for a chance to slobber on its master's fingers. I lowered my gaze in an incredibly nonchalant manner but, to my extreme embarrassment and irritation, I blushed as bright red as a stoplight. I hoped the boy wouldn't notice my infrared cheeks, but I guess he did because he gave me an enormous, exaggerated wink. I wanted to kill myself and disappear between the floorboards—right after I killed *him*, that is.

Then Bonnie, who seemed to have microwaved a thaw on herself, got up and came over to me. "Hi!" she said cheerily. "This is my friend, Kate Clancy, who goes to school with me in L.A. Kate, these are my twin cousins, Barry and Marilyn Williams. They live right here in town in Bluff Point Village."

Barry and Marilyn both gave me their version of the Bennington smile, and I immediately forgot my embarrassment and smiled back at them. As I said before, I don't usually handle myself very well when I'm meeting new people, but for some reason I was sure I was going to be comfortable with these two—well, anyway, I was sure about Marilyn. Her smile was sweet and a bit shy, but with a definite promise of friendship. Barry was another story. There was a certain cocky quality to the way Barry was grinning at me, as if we'd already shared some

35

private joke no one else knew about, and it didn't exactly put me at my ease. In fact it made me want to punch him in the nose.

Anyway there was certainly nothing very threatening about the way the Williams were dressed. Marilyn was wearing a faded, old-but-comfortable cotton sundress, while Barry had on baggy shorts and a too-small Mickey Mouse T-shirt that looked like it had been washed at least a million times. In other words, they were dressed just the way *I* usually dress when I'm not sipping tea above my social station.

I haven't seen too many pairs of twins close up, so I found myself studying Barry and Marilyn, trying to see how much they resembled each other. Their coloring was certainly similar. Unlike their cousin, Bonnie, they both had curly dark hair, olive skin, and big brown eyes. I pondered exactly how they might be related to the Benningtons. Their last name was different, so their father couldn't be a Bennington, but they'd called Eunice and Brewster 'grandma and gramps' so that must mean their mother was a Bennington daughter, which would make her Bonnie's father's sister, or Bonnie's aunt. Whew! I remembered some ancient conversation with Bonnie at school one day when she'd told me about one of her aunt's having died in a car crash about ten years ago. I wondered if Barry's and Marilyn's mother was the same aunt.

Eunice let go of the twins and started peering out into the hallway behind them. "Your father didn't come in with you?" she asked.

Barry tugged at his Mickey Mouse shirt, and Marilyn looked embarrassed and quickly mumbled something about "the shop." Eunice's face fell, and Brewster cleared his throat awkwardly, and immediately my senses came to life again, warning me about another Bennington family skeleton rattling its bones in a closet.

But what could the family secret be? I asked myself. Murder? Arson? Armed robbery?

Shut up! myself broke in. *Keep out of it. Control yourself, or you'll just get into trouble and . . .*

Before I could start another internal fight, Mopsy started talking. "Hello, my dears," she said. "My, how you're both starting to resemble your mother, poor, dear Beatrice." Aha! I thought. 'Beatrice' definitely was the name of the aunt who'd died in the car crash. "My how you've grown since last I saw you."

"But you just saw us yesterday, Mrs. Kingsley," Marilyn reminded her gently. "When Grandma brought you and Mr. Kingsley into the shop."

For some strange reason the exchange of remarks between Marilyn and Mopsy, who was clearly slightly flaky, put me in mind of the kind of conversation I'm always having with my own grandparents, who are definitely *extremely* flaky. I don't know why, but the whole conversation suddenly struck me as hysterically funny. For another strange reason I chose that moment to glance over at Barry. *Big* mistake. Barry was staring right at me, and it was obvious from the way the corner of his mouth was twitching that he had just read my mind, and was *daring* me to laugh right out loud. I didn't give in to the urge however. As quickly as I could, I took a huge gulp of scalding tea—and received third-degree burns on the inside of my mouth.

I probably gasped or something, but fortunately Theo was talking so loudly, no one could hear me. "Yes, indeed!" he boomed. "Charming place, your father's shop. Wonderful antiques, knickknacks, whatnots. Mopsy and I always enjoy poking around in there as we did yesterday. Eunie loves it there too. Why, we practically had to drag her out of the place!"

Barry and Marilyn smiled politely and wandered over to the coffee table and helped themselves to sandwiches and cake. But when Eunice offered them tea, they both said they'd rather have lemonade, and Barry offered to go to the kitchen and get it. At the mention of lemonade, I knew that a cold drink was what I needed more than anything else in the world. Miserably I stared down at my almost-full cup of loathsome tea. Why had I taken it? Why hadn't I asked for something else to drink? Why was I such a jellyfish?

Then a miracle occurred. As Barry passed me on his way out of the living room, he glanced at my brimming cup and then up at my face. "Say, Kate," he said with another conspiratorial wink, "now that you've finished your tea, would you like a lemonade?"

Good grief! Could it be that there was actually a human being lurking behind that more-smart-alecky-than-thou expression? I struggled to think of a devastatingly witty but grateful response to Barry's question, but all I could come up with was a slow, speechless nod—and then another bright blush that was perfectly color-coordinated with my dress. What's the matter with you? I asked myself when he was gone and I'd discreetly hidden my cup behind an asparagus fern. The kid asks if he can get you a lemonade, and you act like a scared rabbit staring down both barrels of a shotgun! What *was* it about those all-knowing, mind-reading eyes that had such a flustering effect on me?

Sigh. While I waited for Barry to come back with my drink, I wandered around the room, half-listening to the grown-ups. The four of them were pretty cute. The two couples were sitting opposite each other on the pair of loveseats, contentedly reminiscing about their childhoods on Beacon Hill in Boston.

I kept walking around the room, hoping for a chance to speak to Bonnie alone, but she was standing by the picture window, talking to Marilyn. When I went over to them, I discovered that the two girls were also reminiscing and laughing about their childhoods. Apparently they used to gang up on Barry in the summers when they were all little kids together. How I would have loved to see that!

By now Bonnie was in her best cheerful form and was telling a story about a big family picnic on some long-lost Fourth of July. "Remember what we did, Marilyn?" she said. She turned to me and started laughing. "You see, Kate, Barry just loves hard-boiled eggs, so when we have picnics, Hettie always packs a few in a little container for him. But this one time, when we were all about eight, Marilyn and I snuck in and took them all out—and then we substituted *raw* eggs!"

"It was all Bonnie's idea," Marilyn added in her gentle quiet voice. "I was terrified we were going to get caught. And we did end up getting into big trouble."

"Marilyn's like that," Bonnie said with an affectionate glance at her cousin. "Always worrying about everything. And honest to a fault."

"Well anyway, tell me what happened," I demanded. "Did Barry get egg all over himself?"

"No, that's the terrible thing. You see, we thought we were safe because everyone else in the family hates hard-boiled eggs. But then at the last minute Great-Uncle Horace from Wellfleet showed up. And before we could stop him, he decided to have an egg. What's worse, for some reason he decided to crack it *on his head!* After that Marilyn confessed on the spot. Eunice and Hettie were both furious with us—and Marilyn was furious with me for dragging her into the whole thing. Remember how upset you were, Marilyn?"

But Marilyn wasn't listening to the story anymore. Instead she was staring fixedly at two objects on a small table right in front of the picture window. I followed her gaze and saw that she was looking at a pair of china statuettes. One was a little boy with a straw hat and the other was a little girl with a big blue droopy bonnet. They were pretty, but so were all the other little knickknacks around the room. I wondered why Marilyn was so fascinated by these particular ones.

Bonnie started telling me some more about Great-Uncle Horace and the egg, but she was interrupted by Eunice, who wanted her to come over and tell Theo and Mopsy something-or-other about life in California. I stayed next to Marilyn and became absorbed in the view of the ocean again, until I became aware that Marilyn wasn't by my side anymore.

When I turned to look at her, she was sidling away, moving closer and closer to the little table with the china girl and boy. She was acting so strange and sneaky, I couldn't help staring. Suddenly an unbelievable thing happened. Marilyn shot out her hand, grabbed up the little girl statuette, and slipped it into her pocket! She reached out again for the little boy, but before she could get him, she accidentally bonked her hip into the table and the whole thing started wobbling. For a fraction of a second the little boy teetered on the edge of the table. Marilyn tried to catch him, but she wasn't fast enough. He pitched off the side and landed with a soft *plip!* on the floor. Fortunately there was a rug under the table, or it would have been smash-up city for him and his straw hat.

Marilyn looked like she wanted to go after the statuette pretty badly, but then seemed to realize she would probably draw attention to what she'd just been doing if she started crawling around on her hands and knees under the furniture. All at once she became elaborately casual.

She turned around, faced the room, and transformed back into the gentle creature she'd been a few minutes ago. She even gave a little yawn, for Pete's sake!

Appalled, I quickly averted my gaze. Marilyn had been so absorbed in committing her crime, I was positive she didn't know I'd been watching her the whole time. In a state of semishock, I looked around to see if anyone else had seen what I'd seen. The Benningtons and Kingsleys were all still enchanted by whatever Bonnie was telling them by the coffee table, and none of them appeared to have noticed a thing. But someone else had. When I glanced at the doorway, I immediately locked eyes with Barry, who had just come in with a trayful of lemonade glasses.

From his expression I knew that he'd seen what his sister had done. I also knew that he'd seen that *I'd* seen. He struggled to put his old cocky look back onto his face, but it was a miserable failure, and from the way the lemonade glasses on the tray shook in front of his Mickey Mouse shirt, I could tell he was rattled. I felt really sorry for him, but I had no way of telling him that, so I just stood there and kept on gawking at him. You can probably guess what happened next. Naturally I started blushing again from head to toe.

6

That night I couldn't sleep at all. My overworked brain just wouldn't stop rehashing the upsetting events of the day. Every time I'd start to drift off, I'd picture sweet, soft-spoken Marilyn's gentle, slender hand. Suddenly her fingers would grow into long, grasping claws reaching out to grab the first china statuette and knocking over the other one. Then I'd sit bolt upright in the bed, listening to my heart thud and wondering what I should have done.

But what *could* I have done? After I'd witnessed the theft, the rest of my first day at Bluff Point Dunes had passed in a kind of migraine-headache blur. When we'd finished with the tea, Eunice and Mopsy had gone up to search the Kingsleys' room, apparently with no success, and the rest of us had gone down for a walk along the beach. It had been truly beautiful there, what with the rugged dunes, the blue sky, the powdery sand, and the majestic schooners on the horizon. In his best tour guide manner, Brewster had given me my very own personalized lecture on local history. I knew it was really nice of him, but I barely heard a word he said. Stuff that would have fascinated me a few hours before had completely lost its interest. All I could do was nod and smile politely as I scurried along the water's edge next to my enthusiastic, Speedy Gonzales of a host.

43

My conscience kept telling me to interrupt Brewster's oration and tell him what I'd seen. In his own breezy way Bonnie's grandfather was really going out of his way to make me feel welcome, and I felt the least he deserved was my honesty. And Eunice, too, of course. She might be upper class, but she'd been the opposite of snooty to me. And after all, I was a guest in their home and I'd just stood by and twiddled my thumbs while someone stole a possession, however tiny and insignificant, right out from under their teacups. But, of course, breaking the news to the Benningtons wouldn't be that easy because the thief was their own granddaughter. Besides, though I hadn't been able to get to know her very well, Marilyn had struck me as a person I could really get to like.

Maybe, I thought, I should say something to Marilyn herself. But what? "Say, I couldn't help noticing how cleverly you snitched that figurine over there, sorry you botched getting the other one? And by the way, are you also responsible for stealing my watch and locket, not to mention Theo's tie clip and Mopsy's bracelet? Just how did you manage it, without being anywhere near the house at the time?"

And then there was the other thing. If I were painfully honest with myself, I had to face up to what was really bothering me in this whole mess: *Barry*. Admit it, Clancy! I said to myself. He's just the kind of wise-guy-with-a-heart-of-gold boy you always fall for. And amazing as it may seem, he actually seems to be at least *remotely* interested in you! So consider this: How do you suppose he'll feel if you squeal on his sister?

The answer was self-evident. Barry would flip out. He was already really upset by what Marilyn had done. During the rest of this afternoon he'd seemed like a different person from the kid who'd swaggered into the living room at teatime. He'd made a few token wisecracks, but his heart just hadn't been in them, and they'd fallen completely flat. Even more significantly, though there'd been countless opportunities, he hadn't even winked at me once! At one point he'd managed to slip around behind me and start muttering something in my ear, but just then Eunice had come up and he'd immediately backed away. Finally, when he and Marilyn were saying good-bye in the front hall before dinner, Barry had managed to whisper. "Listen, Kate. Don't tell anyone. Let me explain first!"

Of course I knew right away what he was talking about. And of course I wanted to do what he said, sucker that I am. But how could I? How could Barry possibly explain away what I'd seen?

Urrrggghhh! I groaned out loud. I was right back where I'd started, all alone with my tortured thoughts. What I really needed now was someone to talk to. But who? I'd tried to corner Bonnie right before dinner. She'd been perfectly willing to chatter about everything under the sun—except when I'd tried to ask her about the famous "last summer" quotations, at which point she shut up like a clam. After dinner she'd said she had a headache and had gone right up to her room. So much for the midnight popcorn pops and giggles we'd planned back in L.A.

45

I wished my cousin Monty were here to talk to. Even my noisy friend, Bobby "Mouth" Berman from L.A., would have been welcome at the moment. Why, I would even have talked to my *mom!*

Thinking of Mom reminded me of how she's always harping on the importance of children getting a good eight hours' sleep every night. Of course I'm not children, but I do like to get *some* sleep, and at this rate I'd be lucky if I got a good eight *minutes'* worth tonight! For one thing my bed was a complete mess. My sheets and blanket were twisted and tangled from all my wild thrashing around, and both sides of my pillow were hot and sweaty. Also my brain was still galloping around in some kind of never-ending horse race. I needed some way of slowing it back down to its normal slow trot.

All right, I told myself. It's time for the ultimate weapon: warm milk. I know what you're thinking. It's pretty nerdy to still be drinking such disgusting stuff at age fourteen, but I was starved for sleep, and warm milk almost never fails to knock me out. Besides it was the middle of the night, and who was to know? I disentangled myself from my bed and crept out of my room.

Bluff Point Dunes Cottage was even more fantastic at night than during the day. Silvery-pale moonbeams washed in through the windows and bathed the hallways with heavenly light. Outside, the waves pounded the shore with a constant roaring beat, reminding me of pirates and sea captains and buried treasure. The whole house even smelled interesting somehow—salty and tangy and exotic. And a little scary.

I tiptoed down the wide front staircase and turned left into the dining room. As I did, my stomach crabbily reminded me that I'd only picked at my dinner. I didn't blame it for being annoyed. It's used to a steady supply of food. But at dinnertime I'd still been too distracted about Marilyn to have much of an appetite. Mopsy and Theo had raved about the food, and Theo had boomed on and on about what a gem of a cook Hettie was and how their old cook, Dora, had been almost as good, and how did the Benningtons always manage to have the best of everything, and so forth. But all I'd done was move the various sauces and globs around on my plate so no one would notice I hadn't eaten a bite.

Okay, okay, okay, I said to my stomach. We'll hunt for some crackers and peanut butter to go with the warm milk. I reached out to push the door into the kitchen. Then I froze in my tracks.

Thud! My heart stopped. Holy cripes! *Thud, thud!* Someone else was walking around in the house; in the living room, behind me, in the dark.

Run! Hide! Shriek! Panic! In my mind's eye I pictured Waldo, stalking me through the halls, swinging his scythe at my neck. All my strained senses screamed at me to duck under the dining room table and wait for morning. But I didn't do it. Some unknown force invaded my body and seized control of me. Inquisitiveness, curiosity, insanity, call it what you want. Something was driving me, forcing me to find out who was prowling the halls in the dead of night.

I held my breath, turned around, and glided back the

way I'd come. A primitive criminal instinct told me to cling to the walls where the sheltering shadows would hide me. My bare feet didn't make a sound on the Persian rugs. I was perfectly quiet. Quiet, that is, until I reached the end of the dining room, stepped out into the front hall, and smashed right into an enormous brass urn filled with antique canes.

Blam! Clatter, clack, crash. The urn banged onto its side and rolled out into the middle of the hall, spilling canes everywhere. More silence. Then *crreak*. What was that? I remembered the sound from this afternoon. The front door creaked when it opened. *Crreak*. And again when it closed. The intruder was leaving.

In two flashes I was in the living room with my nose pressed up against the glass of the picture window. Even I was too smart to follow the stranger outside into the night. But at least I might be able to get a glimpse that would reveal his or her identity.

The moonlight lit up the front lawn like a fluorescent street light on a freeway. Silhouetted against the glowing sky, a dark shadow darted out onto the grass, racing eastward in the direction of the ocean. The figure reached the pretty little white gazebo I'd noticed from my balcony upstairs, then it ran up the gazebo steps, turned around once to glance back at the house, and finally ducked down to hide in the shelter of the ornate railing.

Uh-oh. This was the worst. In the eerie moonlight I hadn't been able to make out the features of the fleeing figure's face. But I *had* been able to see the front of his white T-shirt. Mickey Mouse's big round black ears had stood out as clear as day.

7

For a long moment I stayed by the window, staring out at the gazebo, hoping I'd made a mistake but knowing I couldn't have. It was Barry out there now, and it had been Barry sneaking around in the house a few minutes ago. There was no getting around it, just as there was no getting around Marilyn's stealing the china girl.

I'd assumed that my encounter with the urn would wake up the entire household, but no one else came downstairs so I guessed I'd exaggerated the noise, or else the Benningtons were extra-sound sleepers. Either way, I was saved from having to make up a bunch of believable lies about what I'd seen and heard.

After a while, much older and wiser, I sighed and headed for the stairs. Slowly and quietly I walked through the huge living room and crept back up the front staircase. The upstairs hall was dark and silent. I pulled open the door to my room and slipped inside. As I did, I realized I'd forgotten my warm milk and snack. But that didn't matter. There was no way I was getting any sleep tonight, with or without warm milk.

49

Even though I was absolutely wide awake, I automatically went over to my bed and climbed up on it. I sat on my pillow for a while, clutching my shaky knees and wishing a plane ticket back home would drop into my lap. As I brooded, I was aware of the rhythmic, almost living sound of the surf outside the house. In and out, in and out, like the gentle snoring of some kind of nearby slumbering monster. Was something different about the sound tonight? Did the rhythm always seem that close, as if it was right in the room with me, or . . . or was the sound right in the room with me?

Gulp. For the second time that night my heart stopped. Slowly I turned my head from side to side, scanning the darkness with terrified eyes. As I looked, chills ran up and down my spine, and I knew I'd been right. The 'in and out' I was hearing wasn't the sound of the surf at all. It was the sound of human breathing in this very same room!

I couldn't see anyone, but I knew I had to get out of there. Fast! Go out in the hall. Or better yet, go through the bathroom, into Bonnie's room. As silently as I could, I slung my body sideways and pointed my feet toward the floor. But I guess I wasn't silent enough. As I moved, something else moved too. *Right next to me on the bed!*

I closed my eyes and screamed. I tried to jump off the bed, but a hand grabbed my arm. When I opened my frightened eyes, I was gazing right into Bonnie's face.

"Kate, what's wrong?"

"Look out! In the bed! Something moved! I . . ." My

voice was so high and hysterical, I sounded like a manic Minnie Mouse.

As she listened to me, Bonnie's eyes widened in her pale blur of a face. Then those same eyes crinkled up as she laughed out loud. "Kate!" she said. "That was *me* in the bed. I came in here to talk to you, and I lay down to wait and I guess I fell asleep. But where were you, anyway?"

"Uh . . . I went downstairs for a snack."

"Well, I'm sorry if I scared you."

We sat quietly a minute while my breathing slowly returned to its normal speed. Then I turned and peered through the darkness at my friend. "Uh . . . I'm really happy to see you and everything, Bonnie," I said. "But what exactly are you doing in here? I mean, it's the middle of the night!"

Bonnie's long, sad sigh was worthy of a surfacing whale blowing off steam on top of the water. "I guess I came in here to apologize," she said at last.

"Apologize?" I said. "For what?"

"For inviting you to come here with me. I should have been more honest with you from the start. You see, last summer . . ." She broke off and took a deep breath.

Aha! I thought. "Last summer" again. Finally I was getting to hear the terrible secret.

"Last summer," Bonnie went on, "there was a burglary at Bluff Point Dunes Cottage."

Given the amount of criminal activity I'd observed in just one day here, I would have been surprised if there *hadn't* been a robbery at Bluff Point Dunes Cottage last summer! But I wanted to keep Bonnie talking. "That's horrifying, Bonnie! What happened?"

"Mopsy's pearl necklace was stolen, right out of her room in the middle of the night!"

"That's horrifying," I said again. Had Barry and Marilyn done *that*? "Mopsy certainly has a lot of jewelry."

"Of course she does. Except for the Benningtons, her family are just about the richest people in Boston—or at least they used to be anyway, though I think I heard they had some losses."

"Were the pearls ever recovered? And did they catch the people . . . er, person . . . who did it?"

"Well, no . . . but . . . you see, there's something else about the burglary that . . . ," Bonnie broke off in mid-sentence, and heaved another sigh. "I can't tell you anything else," she said. "And anyway, I just don't believe it."

Naturally enough I wanted to scream with frustration at being cut off mid-secret, but I didn't think Bonnie could be pushed any further right then. So instead I reached out and patted my friend on the arm. "Actually I may know a little more about all this than you think I do, Bonnie."

She dabbed at her eye with her pajama sleeve. "Well if that's true, then you know there's nothing I can do about it." I guessed I knew what she meant. Squealing on her own cousins would be awkward and embarrassing for everyone. "I . . . I'm so sorry about all this, Kate," Bonnie was saying. "Do you want to go home?"

Well, that's just what I'd been thinking about a few minutes ago. But now my conscience spoke out loudly. "Of course I don't want to go home, Bonnie!" I said. "This is a terrific place, and I'm glad you invited me." My jolly Girl Scout leader voice bounced off the walls in the dark room. But corny as it was the act seemed to cheer Bonnie right up. Even through the dark I could see those beautiful teeth gleaming like the stars on the Hollywood Boulevard sidewalk. She reached out both arms and gave me a little hug.

"Thanks, Kate!" she said. "You've already made me feel a lot happier. You know what? It *was* a good idea to bring you here. And you'll see. We will have fun! We'll go swimming, and play tennis, and dress up for the big Fourth of July picnic and . . ." She interrupted herself with a big yawn. "And now we'd both better get some sleep. Barry and Marilyn are coming over for tennis tomorrow after breakfast, so we need all the rest we can get!"

She said good night, and my bewildered eyes watched her bounce over to the bathroom and go back to her own room. Then I flopped my head down on my pillow. Terrific, I thought. I'd cheered Bonnie up so much that now she'd be able to get a good night's sleep. I, on the other hand, was more confused than ever about what was going on at Bluff Point Dunes. I mean, here I was being all sympathetic about Bonnie's anxieties about her criminal cousins, and then out of the blue she refers to Barry and Marilyn as if they're her best friends!

Is Bonnie crazy or what, Clancy? I asked myself as I stared up at the dark ceiling. Or are *you* the one?

53

8

The morning sunrise woke me up, flooding in through the windows and illuminating my whole room. I'd never seen such a bright light in my life, and so early in the morning! I couldn't look at my missing watch, but a little wind-up clock by the bed said it was only 5:30. I'm not usually an early riser, but this time I was glad for the excuse to sit up and get out of bed.

I crossed the room to the double windows and went out onto the balcony. If possible, the view was even more spectacular than yesterday. The big glowing sun created a broad orange and red highway on the water, and giant seagulls swooped and squawked back and forth across the shimmering lanes of light. It was so beautiful, it almost made me believe that nothing bad could exist in this place and that I'd dreamed everything that had happened last night. But when my eyes came to rest on the little white gazebo near the beach stairs, I knew there was no getting away from the truth. It had all been real.

I sighed and leaned both elbows on the railing. Then I noticed my poor, sickly geranium and remembered I'd never gotten around to watering it yesterday. By now I was pretty sure it was dead, but it couldn't hurt to give it a drink. I went to the bathroom, came back with some water, and dumped it into the clay pot.

After that good deed I decided I might as well get dressed and go outside. I hadn't even bothered to unpack last night, so my clothes were all kind of tangled by now. I shook out the most unwrinkled shorts and T-shirt I could find and pulled them on. Then, without putting on my noisy sandals, I went downstairs, out the back door, across the sandy path, and onto the lawn.

The grass was cool and wet on my bare feet, and the early morning sea air smelled fishy and invigorating. If I were into exercise, I would have jogged on down to the beach and run five miles on the sand. Instead I wandered over to the tiny white gazebo and went up the steps.

It was a pretty little building, though actually it wasn't a building at all, but just a raised round floor and some curved benches surrounded by railings. It reminded me of the little canopy thing on top of the wedding cake at my cousin Norma's wedding. The curlicued roof was made out of bent pieces of wood woven together in a delicate lacy pattern. Adorable, but definitely not a place to go for shelter during a rainstorm.

It definitely was, on the other hand, a perfect place to sit and drink in the view of the ocean. I wiped some of the dew off one of the wooden seats and sat down. Ouch! My tailbone smashed into something pointed and painful sticking up out of the back of the bench. I dug around behind me, and my searching fingers discovered the top of a hard, smooth little object that felt as if it were made out of glass.

I turned around and got down on my hands and knees

for a better look. Then, from a crack at the back of the bench, I pulled out the statuette of the little china boy Marilyn had knocked over in the living room yesterday. The part I'd sat on was the edge of the boy's hat, and it was just lucky for him my weight hadn't snapped his tiny head right off.

A new wave of confusion washed over me, but I didn't have much time to swim around in it. *Brrraaccckk!* Some kind of noisy motor sputtered, coughed, and died right in my ear. The sound was so close! Was someone spying on me? Without thinking, I slipped the china boy into my pocket and leaped to my feet.

Yikes! I stifled a scream. Waldo's face was about half an inch away from my own! The short man thrust his chin over the gazebo railing, his ugly features screwed up in an expression of rage and suspicion. "What you think you're doing snoopin' around out here?" he growled at me.

Outrage gave me courage. "Snooping around!" I repeated indignantly. "What are you talking about . . . ?" But my sharp words were drowned out by another loud *brrrraaccckk* as Waldo leaned down and yanked hard at something at his feet. This time the motor vroomed into action, and I realized the gardener had just started up the lawn mower—not the chain saw I'd been dreading.

With his powerful, stumpy hands he seized both handles of the mower and viciously attacked a patch of long grass. It wasn't hard to conjure up a picture of those hands seizing my neck in exactly the same way. As fast as I could, I scooted down the gazebo steps and darted back toward the house.

"This time," I said to myself, "I'm telling." No one could convince me I'd imagined the threatening look on Waldo's face. I didn't know why, but he'd deliberately been trying to scare me again. And again he'd succeeded very well!

I ran into Eunice and Brewster coming out the front door of the house. They were both dressed in sporty designer sweat suits, and they were holding hands. "Good morning, Kate dear!" Brewster said. He stopped on the sandy path and started doing stretching exercises. "Isn't it a marvelous day? We're just off for our little run. Would you care to join us?" Without pausing to hear my answer, he stopped stretching and charged off down the road at a very ungrandfatherly speed.

Eunice, in her usual kindhearted way, was more observant. She gave me a look of concern. From the way my mouth was hanging open, she probably could deduce I wanted to say something. "Are you well, Kate dear?" she asked. "Did you sleep poorly?"

I finally stopped panting. "Waldo," I stammered, waving a hand back toward the gazebo. "With the lawn-mower . . . over there!"

"You mean he's already hard at work?" Eunice said with a delighted laugh. "He's a wonder, isn't he? Such a darling, and so loyal to us, though of course we don't deserve it. Why, we just couldn't manage without Waldo and Hettie!"

Ulp. Darling Waldo! Was Eunice deliberately being slow on the uptake, or was she just being like Bonnie, who always saw the best in people—in spite of all the awful things they did? In either case, how could I complain about the man after the glowing tribute she'd just given him? I forced my tirade back down my throat like some kind of large, loathsome pill. As I swallowed, I remembered Waldo's sudden change-of-face when Bonnie, the little Bonnet, had turned up in my room yesterday. I concluded that although the gardener appeared to hate everyone in the world, particularly me, he actually loved the Benningtons in his own primitive style. Somehow, incredible as it seems, he must have thought I was some kind of threat to them.

As I mused on all this, Eunice gazed down the road after Brewster. "The madman sets himself too fast a pace," she said fondly. "If I leave now, I can just catch up with him when he tapers off to an exhausted walk at the end of the drive. I'll see you later, my dear." With a little wave, she trotted off onto the dirt road that led down the dune. "Breakfast is at nine, Kate!" she called back in her ringing voice.

I stood where I was, looking after her until I couldn't see her anymore. On the one hand, I was sorry I hadn't made her listen to me about Waldo, but on the other hand, I just hadn't been able to dump all over the loyal gardener the Benningtons loved so much. It was hard to imagine deliberately doing anything to upset Eunice. Even though she lived in a world of pearl-handled knives and china teacups, she was still one of the most genuinely nice, kind people I'd ever met. If I could adopt another grandmother, it would definitely be her.

Ah, me. It was all so confusing. As I padded on my bare feet into the house, I glanced at my wrist, and felt a new pang over the loss of my Statue of Liberty watch. A grandfather clock in the front hall said it was only 6:45 A.M. Over two more hours to go until breakfast!

Forget it! growled my stomach. *I'm not waiting. Go into the kitchen and get me something. Now!*

Yes, master. Like a hardworking serf, I headed toward the dining room. With a slight shock, I noticed that someone had picked up my brass urn and replaced the collection of canes I'd spilled. I'd forgotten all about it last night.

Maybe they thought the wind blew the urn over, I thought. Or if I'm lucky, there's a cat or a do . . . I stopped thinking in mid-word. Low, anxious conversation was coming from the kitchen. Shamelessly I pressed my ear against the door to listen.

"I don't think it can be true!" a concerned woman's voice was saying, ". . . even though Waldo believes it!"

A lower, quieter voice answered the woman, but I couldn't hear what it was saying. Then the first voice started up again. ". . . girl . . . California seems nice . . . Waldo says . . . snoopy!" I realized the angry woman in the kitchen was talking about me!

Snoopy! she'd said. The nerve of that Waldo, spreading rumors about me! But I didn't have time to work up into

59

a satisfying rage because at that instant, the kitchen door swung open in my direction, banging me right on my snoopy ear. I cried out and jumped backward, tears of pain springing to my eyes. Then a strong hand caught my arm, and I was staring up at Hettie's gaunt face.

Whoever she'd been talking to came forward and peered at me over Hettie's shoulder. "Oh, hi, Kate," Barry said with a big grin. "I was wondering when you'd ever get up. Come on in the kitchen and have a donut with us!"

9

I hesitated for a fraction of a second. In that instant my mental VCR rewound itself and played back the picture of Barry skulking across the lawn to the gazebo in the dead of night. Definitely a dangerous criminal. I opened my mouth to refuse his offer.

"Sure!" I said. "I'm starving." I bopped right on into the kitchen with him, sat down at the butcher-block table, and helped myself to a gigantic, sugary cinnamon donut. You're probably wondering what came over me. I could say my detective reflexes were activated, and I was in search of more clues. I could say I just wasn't able to resist Barry's big brown eyes and devilish grin, and I was in search of romance and adventure. And I could say

I was truly hungry, and I was in search of a big fat donut!

Anyway, as soon as we sat down, Barry jumped back up again to pour me a glass of freshly squeezed orange juice from a pitcher on the counter. Hettie strode into the kitchen after us and stood with her hands on her hips, looking mournfully first at Barry and then at me. Finally, though, she gave Barry an exasperated but affectionate smile. She shrugged her shoulders, yanked some copper pots off one of the hanging racks, and began moving them around on the big black stove.

Barry glanced at Hettie and winked at me, and for once, I didn't turn red. As I munched on my crunchy-on-the-outside, soft-on-the-inside donut, I wondered what exactly he was doing here. Yesterday he and Marilyn had come to the front door and politely rung the bell as if a visit to this house were a big, formal deal to them. Last night he'd been sneaking around the halls in the shadow of darkness. But today Barry was lounging around with his feet on the kitchen table at 7:00 A.M. like he owned the place.

"So," he said, "at last I get to meet a real-live California girl who isn't my cousin. You're from L.A., right?"

My mouth was so stuffed, I couldn't talk, but I did manage one of my clever nods.

"We went out there when we were little kids when my mom was still alive," he went on. "I still have the Mickey Mouse T-shirt we got on that trip. It's my best shirt."

No kidding, I thought. You wore it yesterday, for

Pete's sake! Not to mention last night in the moonlight.

Barry started to say something else, but Hettie interrupted him with a long siege of pot clanging. Barry glanced at her with a wry expression, and then turned back to me and shrugged. "My dad says he might take us out there again before school starts if the shop makes enough money off the simple-minded summer people this season."

"*MMMmmnguh,*" responded my crumb-filled mouth. There was a long silence while I struggled to come up with something else to say. There were a lot of things I *wanted* to say, of course, like "Why wouldn't your father come into the house yesterday?" or "Why did your sister steal the china girl from the living room?" or "Why were you sneaking around the cottage last night?" or "Why do both Hettie and Waldo resent my very existence?" But with Hettie right there, I didn't feel as if I could ask about any of those things. In fact, as is pretty common with me and boys, I couldn't think of a thing I *could* ask Barry about! Finally though, I remembered something safe. I swallowed the last of my donut, reached for another, and said, "Bonnie says you and Marilyn are coming over for tennis after breakfast."

Barry paused for a gulp of juice before he answered. "Ah yes, tennis," he sighed. "Do you play?"

Now I did turn red. The subject wasn't safe after all. My tennis game is awful. In fact all my games are awful, except maybe for Candyland. But I hated to admit it. People like the Benningtons are born with silver tennis racquets in their fists. They probably think anyone who doesn't feel the game is "marvelously exhilarating" is some kind of total freak.

Still it was better to confess now than be humiliated on the courts later. I started to speak, but Barry spoke first. "Because," he continued, "I hate it! I'd do almost anything to get out of playing. In fact I was hoping maybe you'd want to bike up to Provincetown with me instead and hang out for a while and maybe check out the local eateries. That is unless you were really looking forward to a smashing round of doubles with Mopsy and Theo."

Well Barry had just offered me a great way of avoiding an embarrassing tennis game, but of course I couldn't accept his offer. After all I was Bonnie's guest, and it wouldn't be right to make plans with her cousin on the second day of my visit. More importantly I reminded myself, Barry's sister was a thief—and so was Barry! It might be okay to sit around talking in the kitchen, but a long bike trip with him didn't seem like a good idea.

For the second time that morning I opened my mouth to refuse. "That sounds terrific, Barry," I said. "When do you want to go?" Okay, okay, so I did it again. So what's the big deal? Haven't *you* ever changed your mind before?

During our whole conversation Hettie had been smashing pots nonstop, but as I said I'd go to Provincetown with Barry, she smacked down a saucepan so hard it actually bounced off the burner and clattered onto the floor, spattering melted butter everywhere. She turned around and started to say something when footsteps could be heard in the dining room.

All at once her face completely changed. She gave Barry a warning look, and strode across the kitchen to yank open the back door to the outside. Barry pushed back his chair, grabbed another donut, and jumped to his feet. As he hurried out the door, he gave me one last wink. "Eleven o'clock, Kate," he whispered. "On the beach. Be there or be square!"

As Barry went out that door, Theo Kingsley bounced in through the other. "Morning, all!" he trumpeted. "Wondered if I could get a cuppa to take up to Mopsy. Hold her over till breakfast, don't you know?"

I thought it was sweet of Theo to be fetching coffee for his bride at this hour of the morning, but Hettie didn't seem to be moved. She took a mug from a shelf, trudged over to a big percolator, and sloshed out a steaming hot cup. She acted as if her thoughts were someplace else entirely. Her long face looked gaunt, tired, and most of all *anxious*. But what, I asked myself, did Hettie have to be so excessively worried about?

10

Anyway, in spite of her high anxiety level Hettie managed to produce an incredible amount of food, including oatmeal, bacon and sausages, eggs with some kind of yellow sauce, bran muffins, and strawberries and cream. The food was served in covered silver dishes arranged on the sideboard in the dining room, and we were all supposed to pick up a plate (pre-heated, of course) and choose what we wanted.

I didn't take too much since I was still pretty full of cinnamon donuts. I noticed Eunice and Brewster didn't eat a lot either, just a couple of bran muffins and a small bowl of berries each. But Theo Kingsley ate quite a bit. After he'd had second helpings of everything, he asked if he could take a tray up to Mopsy. Eunice looked up from her muffin in concern. "Mopsy's not ill, is she Theo?"

"Oh, no, no, no, Eunice, love! The poor darling just didn't sleep that well last night . . . a bit worried, you know. About things."

He didn't elaborate, but from the looks on all the Bennington faces, I could tell they thought he was referring to her missing jewelry. I agreed with them. No one had time to make any comment about it though, because at that point, smiling, shy Marilyn showed up at the front door, looking willowy and angelic in her tennis whites—and not the slightest bit like a burglar. Bonnie, who was already wearing her own neat little tennis outfit, asked me if I wanted to go upstairs and change into mine (which, of course, is nonexistent). I'd put off telling Bonnie I'd already made my own plans, but when I finally did babble out that Barry and I were biking to Provincetown, she acted as if it was the most normal thing in the world and even recommended a restaurant for lunch. It struck me again that Bonnie and I might have had a few wires crossed during our conversation in the dark last night.

Anyway, 11:00 A.M. found me carefully picking my way down the long, steep stairs to the beach. Barry was already waiting at the bottom, lounging against the wooden railing and drawing pictures with his toes in the sand. He explained that he'd left the bikes about half a mile away, up near the road that we'd be taking to Provincetown.

"I thought we'd stroll along the top of the dunes for a while," he said. "There's a path with a great view. I even brought my binoculars."

I gave him my standard clever nod, and the two of us started up the beach. After a while Barry headed onto a hidden path that led away from the water through some tall grass uphill toward the crest of the dunes. We didn't say anything as we climbed, though believe me my brain was busily supplying more and more questions for me to ask Barry about the mysteries at Bluff Point Dunes.

Just before we reached the top of the hill, my escort

cleared his throat. "Ah . . . Kate?" he said. "You're probably wondering why Hettie threw me out of the kitchen like that this morning."

"Well, yes, I was a little curious," I said. Actually I was *extremely* curious.

"Well it's a long sad story," he said, "so get out your handkerchief. You see Marilyn and I love coming up to the cottage to see Grandma and Gramps. We both feel pretty close to Hettie, too, since she used to be a kind of nanny to our mom—and to us, too, when we were little. To us Hettie is sort of like a second grandmother, or a friendly aunt we can tell our troubles to. But the thing is that our father doesn't see it that way at all. In fact he doesn't like Marilyn and me showing up at the Dunes cottage all the time, and I didn't want anyone to find me there that early in the morning and then tell Dad about it later."

I was confused. "But he drove you up for tea yesterday. And you were supposed to play tennis with Bonnie this morning."

"Oh, well, he thinks it's okay if we go now and then when we're invited for a specific thing. But he doesn't like me just dropping in and hanging out like we were relatives or something. It's all a big pain, but Marilyn and I try not to rock the family boat if it's at all possible."

He didn't say anything else for a long time. Finally the silence started driving me crazy. "Why?" I asked. "You *are* relatives, so why doesn't your father want you hanging out at the cottage?"

Barry shook his head and grinned halfheartedly. "The

truth is like something from a TV soap opera," he said, "except without commercial interruption. You see, my father thinks that Gramps and Grandma haven't ever approved of him because he's just a local boy and he runs a shop in town. He feels they didn't want my mom to marry him."

"Didn't they?"

"I don't know . . . maybe at the time it was true. My mom was a debutante and everything, and they probably hoped she'd marry someone a little more like them. But that was twenty years ago! My parents had a very happy marriage, and I know Gramps and Grandma want to be friends with my father now, but Dad just won't let them. And he tries to make Marilyn and me keep our distance too."

Well this speech was followed by a long silence sort of like the one in the kitchen this morning. But this silence wasn't awkward because I wasn't struggling to think of anything to say. There wasn't anything *to* say. It was the first serious speech I'd heard Barry make, and I felt sorry for him. Somehow I was sure he knew it.

We'd kept on walking as we'd talked intermittently, and now we came to the top of the dune. Barry turned around and spread both his arms toward the horizon. "Is this a view, or what?" he asked.

It was. The ocean looked more beautiful than ever. But honestly I wasn't really thinking about the view because my fingers wouldn't let me. All morning my hand had kept straying in and out of my pocket, touching the hat of the little china boy. Finally, without really thinking about what I was doing, I grabbed the little guy and pulled him out. When I opened up my hand, the tiny figure sparkled and glinted in the bright light.

Suddenly Barry clutched my arm in a man-of-steel grip. "Where did you find that?" he barked at me. Uh-oh. The wise-guy grin, the laughing eyes, the teasing remarks were gone, and I was staring into the face of a human possessed by rage.

In the space of a millisecond I became acutely, painfully aware of where we were, teetering at the very edge of a rugged, craggy dune, high above a deserted beach. Lonely, isolated, remote, and dangerous. Right there in the hot sun, I broke into a cold sweat. My breath wheezed in and out in short, fitful pants. In short, I was scared out of my mind.

11

Suddenly my fear was submerged by a hot tidal wave of anger. Here I was blissfully developing a mild romantic feeling for Barry, and here he was ferociously digging his fingers into my arm. It just wasn't fair, and I didn't have to stand around and put up with it!

"You know perfectly well where I found the statuette!" I snarled. "In the gazebo, where you left it last night."

Barry's face darkened with fury, but not for long. His anger faded away, and he sighed and shook his head. "I'm sorry, Kate," he said, letting go of my arm. "I'm acting like a real jerk. And please don't tell me I always act like a jerk! This whole thing is making me crazy. And careless too. I can't believe I lost that figurine in the gazebo after all the trouble I took getting it. I guess I'll have to give up my ambition of being a career thief."

For once his humor left me cold. "*Very* amusing!" I said nastily. "Maybe you should take thief lessons from your sister, Marilyn!"

Barry smiled ruefully. "I'm sorry you saw that incident in the living room," he said. "If you knew Marilyn a little better, you'd know the kind of courage it took for her to do what she did. And I wish I could give you a good explanation for it. But I can't."

"Does this have something to do with the burglary last summer?" I asked.

Barry looked surprised. "So Bonnie told you about it?"

"Yes, she did," I said firmly. "All about it." Only a half-lie, I told myself guiltily.

"Well then you know what we figured out the morning after the burglary," he said.

"Uh, sure," I said. Please, *please* keep talking, Barry! I thought. You're right on the verge of telling me something important.

But Barry was eyeing the figurine in my hand. "What are you going to do with our little friend now, anyway?" he asked casually. Despite his anti-crook declaration, he almost looked as if he were thinking of snatching it away from me again.

"I . . . I'm not sure," I said. I started to stuff the little china boy back in my pocket when Barry grabbed my arm again—though this time he was a lot more gentle. "Please," he said. "Please. Be careful with it! It's worth . . . well, more than a round trip from here to Disneyland."

Oh, dear. And I'd actually *sat* on the thing! I looked around in confusion. Now that I knew the figurine was really valuable, I was sure I was about to break it immediately.

Barry read my mind. "I know what you can do," he said. "There's a carrying case hooked onto Marilyn's bike. It's just like a miniature padded cell. You can put the little beggar in there till you get back home. That is if you still want to ride bikes with me after all this."

In what was getting to be my usual habit, I opened my mouth to say, "No, I wouldn't dream of going with you," and promptly said, "Sure, I still want to go." My dad calls this kind of behavior going with your guts instead of your gray matter. Dad can be truly gross, but in this case I guess the shoe fit—or whatever that dumb old saying is.

Now Barry was grinning his smug, self-satisfied, ir-resistible grin and looking at his watch. "We'd better get going to P-town," he said. "But first you should check out the view through my binoculars." He pointed

71

back in the direction we'd come. "If you look down that way, you can see Bluff Point Dunes Cottage."

With my free hand, I slipped the strap of the binoculars around my neck and aimed them the way he'd said. After seeing double for a while, I finally got the cottage in focus. "Wow!" I cried. "It's like we're only a few feet away!" The binoculars zoomed in and brought the front of the house right up close. I could see all the balconies and all the geraniums. "Say! There's my own room. I recognize my dead plant."

I studied the house for a moment longer. "Barry," I said after a while, "I think there's someone *in* my room. Someone with white hair. Is it Eunice . . . no! I think it's Brewster! But what would he be doing in my room?"

Barry yanked the binoculars away from my face so fast, I almost got whiplash. "Probably changing the sheets," he said, lifting the strap back up over my head. "Come on. We'd better get going. We have a long bike ride up ahead."

Naturally I knew Barry was giving me the first stupid explanation that popped into his mind. Did he think I was a complete idiot? Even I knew that Hettie was the one who changed the sheets at Bluff Point Dunes. Brewster Bennington would never be in my room for that reason.

But I'd already overspent my emotional allowance, and I just couldn't work up the strength to argue about it. And anyway, what could I do about it from here? Nothing! So I might as well relax and enjoy myself.

With that thought, I followed Barry through the tall grass to a small grove of trees where he'd parked our bikes. I was a little worried about putting the china boy in the carrying case, but I figured I didn't have much choice. I carefully tucked him into a snug little compartment, and a few minutes later we were on the road to Provincetown.

The bike ride took about an hour. I knew my muscles would make me sorry for all the strain tomorrow, but today the exercise actually felt good. The sun was shining and the pine trees along the way smelled wonderful. As we sped down the road, I felt like a freewheeling bird, flying along on top of a salty sea breeze.

Provincetown turned out to be amazing in its own strange way. It was a funny mix of quaint old sea cottages side by side with bizarre little shops selling weird gadgets like they have on Hollywood Boulevard. The town was small but busy, and absolutely packed with tourists and lots of other strange characters. With me carefully clinging to the carrying case from the bike, we wandered up and down the narrow streets, gaping in windows and looking at all the stuff. I bought some post cards, a Cape Cod towel for my dad, and a seashell necklace for my mom. It was terribly tacky, but I knew she'd love it anyway.

We ended up having lunch at a little clam bar with great greasy onion rings and chocolate milk shakes. By now I felt so comfortable with Barry, I was actually able to relax and enjoy my favorite activity—eating junk food.

Every now and then my brain would remind me that I was being really stupid spending all this time with Barry when I was still totally in the dark about what he and his sister were up to. But I couldn't help myself. He was about the funniest boy I'd ever met, and I didn't want to spoil the afternoon by asking a bunch of questions I knew he'd refuse to answer anyway.

After we shared one more order of onion rings, Barry looked at his watch again. "We have to hit the trail for home soon, pardner," he said in a cornball John Wayne imitation. "But first I want to take you to this great place with giant chocolate chip cookies."

Oh, joy! Rapture! We'd just stuffed ourselves, and now the kid was suggesting going someplace else for more food. Truly a man after my own heart!

We bid the clam bar a fond good-bye, and Barry led me to a tiny little out-of-the-way side street. We passed a law office (Fenster, Fenster, and Dogwood, etc.), an insurance office (World Life Property, Inc.), a boutique that sold antique clothes (Buy Gone Era), and a place that looked like a pawn shop from an old movie. Then the wonderful aroma of baking cookies filled our noses.

"We made it!" Barry said. "Cookie Heaven." He started to pull open the door of the tiny bakeshop, when I suddenly became aware of another smell, mixing in with the yummy one. Uh-oh. The flower scent again. I couldn't believe the soap odor had lasted since yesterday's shower, but apparently it had, or else maybe the exertion of the bike ride had released its smelly powers one more

74

time. I prayed everyone around me hadn't been gagging on Eau de Lavender soap all day, but there wasn't a lot I could do about it now.

Anyway Barry didn't seem to notice. He was talking to someone just behind my left shoulder. "Fancy meeting you here, Mr. Kingsley," he said.

I turned around and saw Theo Kingsley standing only a few inches behind me. He seemed just as surprised to see us as we were to see him. "Hello there, muh boy!" he said. "And to you, too, muh dear! Enjoying yourselves in Provincetown, are you?"

"We were just about to load up on cookies," Barry said, indicating the shop.

"So was I!" Theo said enthusiastically. "My favorite place! Always stop in here when Mopsy comes up to have her hair done."

Well I was afraid it would take some of the fun out of our cookie binge to have to indulge in it with Theo, but actually he turned out to be pretty much of a riot. He told us some stories about himself and Mopsy and Eunice and Brewster when they were all rich kids together in Boston, and we laughed so hard we almost choked on our chocolate chips. He was definitely one of those people who made the olden days sound like the best time to have been alive. And he didn't seem to have much use for the way things were today. I remembered Mopsy saying pretty much the same kind of thing in the living room the first time I met her.

As I bit into my third king-sized cookie, I reflected

about the way that the Kingsleys seemed to move in with the Benningtons in the summers now that they no longer owned their own cottage. Their oldest and dearest friends, Eunice had said. I wondered whom *my* oldest and dearest friends would be when I reached their age.

Anyway after eating about a thousand cookies each, we said good-bye to Theo and left the shop. As we went down the front steps, I realized I'd left Marilyn's carrying case with its precious cargo under the little table in the cookie shop. Horrified, I raced back inside, certain the case had already been stolen. Fortunately, however, it was still there, wedged under my chair. I grabbed it up, said another good-bye to Theo, who was still finishing his coffee, and hurried outside again.

Barry and I walked through town to the rack where we'd chained our bikes and loaded my packages onto the back of Barry's bike for the ride home. The return trip to Bluff Point Dunes took slightly longer than the way there, and by the time we got to the turn-off for the Benningtons' cottage, dark thunderclouds were threatening overhead. As we puffed our way up the last steep hilly road, a few big drops splatted down on our noses. Of course Barry got to the top way ahead of me. By the time I pulled up next to him, I was gulping for air, barely clinging to life. To my amazement, when I glanced at Barry's face, he looked even worse!

"That hill's really a drag, isn't it?" I began. "Next time I'm . . ."

I stopped when I realized my companion wasn't listening to a word I was saying. He was staring straight ahead in the direction of the house. I stared, too, and then I gasped out loud. A big black police car blocked the driveway. Its light was flashing, and its transmitter was buzzing and whizzing like a bunch of radioactive bees. Something terrible had happened at Bluff Point Dunes!

12

Barry and I left our bikes on the driveway and ran hand-in-hand into the house. Inside we found a living room full of people. Mopsy Kingsley was the center of attention. She was lying on one of the little couches, dabbing at her eyes and making little moaning sounds. Everyone else—Hettie, Waldo, Brewster, Eunice, Bonnie, Marilyn—was grouped in a circle around her.

I was surprised to see Mopsy because I thought Theo had said she was in Provincetown having her hair done. But I must have misunderstood him, because there she was with her red eyes and puffy face and her hair just as wispy and flyaway as always. In fact she looked terrible, sort of like Red Riding Hood's grandmother right before the wolf tossed her out of her sickbed. She looked so pathetic, I wanted to run over and give her a comforting hug, but just then she started talking.

"Eunice dear," she said. "Eunice dear. I'm so sorry to bring all this trouble upon you. But this time I'm positive I'm not being addlepated. I actually have proof."

"Proof of what, Mopsy?" Bonnie asked in a shaky voice. I gave my friend a quick glance and saw to my dismay that she looked almost as terrible as Mopsy.

"Proof that . . . well, that *it* has happened again. You see, even though I didn't say so, I was very disturbed by Eunice's suggestion that I might merely have misplaced my bracelet yesterday. I mean, my dears, if I've become *that* absentminded, I might as well take to my bed. So this time I decided to make sure of what was really happening. Oh, my, but a person just isn't safe nowadays."

She paused to snuffle pitifully into her hanky. Then she went on. "I put my diamond brooch into my jewelry box this morning at 10:30 A.M. when I came downstairs. After I closed the box, I had an inspiration. I decided to place a hair across the crack, just the way the detectives always do in the movies. I was sure nothing would come of it. But just now when I looked at the box, the hair was gone, and so was my brooch! Oh, Eunice, I'm so sorry."

Brewster looked perturbed and began striding back and forth on the carpet at his standard speed-of-lightning pace. Eunice showed her usual concern for another human being's suffering. She sat down beside Mopsy on the couch and took her friend's hand between her own. "Don't carry on so, Mopsy," she said soothingly. "After all I'm not the one who's been robbed. You are. If in fact you have been robbed. Why, I was up in your room myself this morning, and I didn't notice a thing amiss. And besides, I'd hardly call a missing hair proof of a robbery, Mopsy. Hettie probably swept it away with her feather duster. And you easily could have moved the brooch yourself and put it someplace else and then just forgotten all about it and . . ."

"No, no, no, my dear," Mopsy interrupted. "First of all, as for Hettie dusting, I accidentally spilled some powder in front of the jewelry box this morning, and I'm sorry to say it's still there." This speech made Hettie start wringing her big hands together, and then Waldo stepped forward. "Hettie didn't have time to dust the rooms yet," he said fiercely. "She was in town with me all day, helping with the shopping." Apparently Waldo's ferocious loyalty extended to his wife as well as to the members of the Bennington family.

Mopsy blew her nose and went on in her shaky, whispery voice. "I wish I could believe I moved the brooch myself and forgot, but as Bonnie and Marilyn can tell you, I haven't been back to my room since I came downstairs this morning!"

Bonnie and Marilyn, whose faces were both a sickly shade of green, exchanged quick glances and then nodded up and down. I couldn't figure out how they'd become witnesses as to where Mopsy had been all morning since I'd thought they were playing tennis, but before I could make a start on solving this puzzle, Brewster spoke up in his authoritarian manner. "I can see this has all been very distressing for you, Mopsy," he said. "But I'm sure that, if you had only come to me instead of calling in the police without consulting me . . ."

"I did it to protect . . . your family, Brewster. Why, to protect all of us! The police can *prove* an intruder has come into your home!"

I could see Eunice and Brewster didn't want the police called in, but that just didn't make sense to me. Why didn't they want the police to catch the intruder? I mean, if Mopsy's brooch was really worth a lot of money, you'd think everyone would want to catch the thief as fast as possible, particularly if it turned out to be the same thief who'd stolen the pearls last summer. Calling in the police seemed like the best way to find the thief. Unless, that is, you had some secret reason for not wanting him or her found. Hadn't Bonnie said there was "something else" about last summer's burglary? Something she couldn't tell me?

Crack! A flash of lightning lit up the room. Boom! A tremendous clap of thunder rocked the house—and me too. Immediately afterward a voice spoke from a corner of the room, and I almost jumped right out of my skin.

"Mrs. Kingsley did the right thing. The sooner we're called in, the better we're able to do our job."

I turned around and peered into the shadows to see who was speaking. A tall, pale man with tired, thoughtful eyes came forward into the light. He wasn't wearing a uniform, but from the official way he was talking, he was obviously a policeman.

Behind us in the hall the front door creaked open, and a soggy Theo Kingsley bounced into the room. "'Lo, all!" he began. "Rainin' cats and . . ." He caught sight of the crowd around his wife and broke off in mid-fragment. Then he rushed to Mopsy's side, got down on his knees, and clutched her hand. "What's up, pet? Are you all right?" As usual, I was touched by his concern for his childhood sweetheart.

"Oh, Theo!" Mopsy wailed. "The most dreadful thing happened while you were away. And now I'm very much afraid I've made Eunice and Brewster angry with me."

Theo's loud voice became amazingly soft as he brushed the hair off his wife's forehead and made soothing, sympathetic noises. Mopsy was obviously about to break down in tears again, but before she could the plainclothes policeman interrupted her. "Excuse me, Mrs. Kingsley," he said. "I know you want to talk to your husband, but I'm going to conduct some individual interviews in the dining area, and I need to get started." He scanned the room, looking for his first victim, and though I was sure he wouldn't pick me, I wrestled with a sudden urge to bolt out the front door. Then to my absolute horror the man's searchlight gaze stopped on my face. "Won't you come across the hall with me please, Miss?" he asked.

Suddenly, vital organs started shifting and stirring inside me. My heart and lungs were sinking fast, but my stomach was swiftly surging up to meet them. Soon everything would smash together, and I'd explode into a million pieces on the rug. Sickening, but still better than being grilled by the police. Why you, Clancy? Why you? I asked myself in a total state of panic. Can't you throw up or something? Or collapse into a coma on the couch?

But as usual, my body stubbornly refused to listen to my brain, and all I did was meekly trail after the policeman as he marched across the hall. To make matters worse, as I left, I was keenly aware of multiple sets of eyeballs burning holes into my back. I didn't have to turn around to know that a number of people in that room were wondering exactly what I planned to tell the police.

13

Actually we didn't go into the dining room, but rather into the children's dining room, which was more private because it had a big, thick door you could close. I was so frozen with fear, I felt like someone had dumped a snow cone down my back, even though so far the policeman had been pretty nice.

I'd been expecting the man to whip out a set of thumbscrews and a dangling light bulb, but instead he politely introduced himself as Sergeant Schott (which in happier times I might have thought was a funny name for a policeman), and asked me if I wanted something to drink before we sat down.

As a matter of fact, a drink would have been welcome since my throat felt about as dry as Death Valley. But when I opened my mouth to say 'yes,' no sounds came out. It was just as well. My hands were shaking so badly, I'd probably have spilled a drink all over myself.

The two of us sat down on opposite sides of the long, narrow wooden table where little, wealthy, blond Bennington children had been throwing their food around for countless summers. The sergeant had his back to the window, which meant that I was the one who got to stare at the torrents of rain sheeting down from the dark angry sky outside. The weather matched my mood perfectly, and in some mysterious way the sergeant seemed to know it.

"You seem a little nervous," he said. "Any particular reason for that?"

My vocal chords came back to life. "Oh, no," I said in a too-loud, too-bright voice. "It's just that I've never really talked to a policeman before, except if you count the time I got lost at the playground when I was three. You see my mom just turned her back for a minute, and I wandered out the gate right onto Pico Boulevard. Of course, I don't remember any of this, but my mom says . . ."

"*Hrrrrrmmmm!*" Sergeant Schott loudly cleared his throat, abruptly stopping the flood of inane babble gushing from my mouth. Get control of yourself, Clancy! my inner voice screamed to me. If you keep blabbing like that, he'll know you're guilty!

Hold on just a minute! I argued. *I'm not guilty.*

But you feel guilty, don't you? So why don't you just go ahead and confess?

Confess what? I hissed back, wildly wondering if I'd been possessed by some kind of demon. Fortunately, before I could drive myself completely around the bend, Sergeant Schott's calm voice broke in on my deranged thoughts. "The reason I wanted to talk to you first, Miss . . . Clancy, is it?"

"Right. Kate Clancy."

"Miss Clancy," he continued, "is that, according to the list I was given by Mrs. Bennington, you're the only person staying here who isn't either a relative, an employee, or a long-time friend of the family. Is that correct?"

"Well I'm friends with Bonnie," I said. "We go to school together in Los Angeles." My voice sounded pretty calm, but actually I wanted to weep with relief. I'd been sure the sergeant wanted to interrogate me first because he knew I had guilty knowledge. Which, now that I thought of it, I did. Or maybe I did anyway. I wasn't sure about anything around here anymore.

"But you met Mr. and Mrs. Bennington for the first time yesterday afternoon?"

I nodded, and Sergeant Schott scribbled something in a little black notebook. "Now, Miss Clancy," he continued. "Have you noticed anything unusual going on around here? Strangers about the place? Noises in the night? Things disappearing? Any particular person acting suspiciously?"

84

Holy cripes! I'd noticed *all* those things and more! But
. . . my mind's eye focused on an image of the circle of
anxious faces in the living room. I just couldn't squeal
on them. Not yet anyway. Not till I had a better idea
what was going on. "I haven't noticed anything unusual
at all, Sergeant," I said. I tried to use a firm, steady tone,
and I looked the man right in the eye as I spoke. He
stared right back at me. And stared and stared. I did
okay at first, but then my face suddenly turned bright
red.

"Has anyone mentioned any other robberies?" he
asked. "Have you heard any references to a break-in that
took place last summer?"

"No," I half-whispered, half-croaked. When you're
lying through your teeth, it's hard to get the words out.

The sergeant asked me a million more probing questions, and finally I settled on a dumb head-shake as my
best response. Finally he sighed and snapped his notebook
shut. Now his eyes *really* looked tired. For the first time
in my life, I realized policemen are simply plain old
human beings doing their job, just like my father, when
he sells paper supplies, and my mother, when she tickets
airline passengers. I had an urge to throw him a small
scrap of truth, just to make him feel better, but before
I could think of anything harmless enough, he pushed
back his chair.

"All right, Miss Clancy," he said in a resigned tone
of voice. "If you think of anything you do want to tell
me, give me a call down at the police station. There will
probably be an insurance man around the place soon, so

you'll have to answer some more questions. I understand the Kingsleys have heavy policies on most of their jewelry, so naturally the company will conduct its own investigation."

He got to his feet. I did the same thing and then practically ran from the children's dining room. When I burst out into the main dining room, I started for the main stairs but then quickly changed my mind. To get to that stairway, I'd have to pass those inquiring eyes in the living room, and I just couldn't face them right now. I veered to the right, went through the swinging door into the kitchen, and tore up the back stairs to the second floor.

You may be wondering why I was in such a hurry, and I'm not sure I can tell you. All I knew was that I felt terrible, and I wanted to be alone. My insides were a mixed-up jumble of confusion, worry, loneliness, and guilt. I ran into my room, closed the door, and threw myself down on my bed. I needed to sort out my thoughts and feelings, but that could wait. First and foremost, I wanted to have a good, long, self-pitying cry.

While the rain bashed against the windows, I buried my face in my pillow and prepared to weep. But before I got out a single sob, my clenched-up fist felt something hard under the edge of the top sheet. I sat up on my elbow, yanked off the bedcovers, and stared. The bright green face of the Statue of Liberty stared back at me. My beloved missing plastic watch had come home.

14

"Dear Monty," (I wrote to my cousin and best friend in Denver). *"You're not going to believe this, but I've gotten myself mixed up in another mystery. And this one truly is mysterious. Whenever I think I've figured something out, something else happens and I'm right back where I started. I wish you could be here so we could talk about what's going on. But since you're not, I thought writing you a letter might help me sort things out."*

I stopped writing for a minute to chew on my pen and stare out at the storm. Then I glanced down at my newly returned watch and shook my head. I might be a little scatterbrained sometimes, but I'd never believe I'd managed to lose the watch in my bed without realizing it. Besides, where was the locket that had disappeared at the same time?

I went back to my letter. *"First of all, a lot of things have vanished from around this house (which is really a mansion—I wish you could see it!). Some of it's very valuable, and some isn't, and now at least one thing has been returned! Can you make sense of it? I sure can't! One problem is that it seems as if there's no one person who could be taking the stuff. And at least some of the people here seem to be involved in some kind of cover-up or conspiracy. But what exactly are they covering up?*

"Now, so you'll know whom I'm talking about, the people who either live, visit, or work here are: Bonnie Bennington (my friend from home—a really nice kid, though lately I can't get her to talk to me), Eunice and Brewster (her grandparents, but you'd hardly believe it. Eunice looks like a model, but is an angel of a person; Brewster also is very good-looking, and is nice in a breezy, businessman kind of way), Hettie and Waldo (the strange housekeeper and gardener), Barry and Marilyn Williams (Bonnie's cousins—more on them later . . . much more), Mr. Williams (their mysterious, mostly absent father), and Theo and Mopsy Kingsley (the Benningtons' dearest friends, who are a really adorable old couple). Oh, yes. And me (your loving cousin).

"I can't believe that either the Benningtons or the Kingsleys could be thieves, mainly because the idea is so mind-boggling, but also because they don't have any motive because they're all filthy rich—or used to be, anyway, according to Bonnie. Besides, the Kingsleys are three-time victims. Hettie and Waldo seem like a better choice, but they have alibis for this morning when one of the biggest thefts took place, plus Waldo seems to have an almost unnatural devotion to the Benningtons. I haven't met Mr. Williams yet, but apparently he doesn't get along with Eunice and Brewster very well. And now for Barry and Marilyn: Even though I actually saw each one of them take something out of the house, Barry gives the impression that things aren't what they seem to be around here. Also Bonnie said something mysterious about being helpless to do anything. So you can see why I'm totally confused!"

I stopped again and read over what I'd written. When

I came to the part about Barry and Marilyn, a loud alarm bell clanged in my mind. What an imbecile. Yes, I *had* seen Barry take something from the house—the china boy! And I'd left it outside in the rain!

I threw my pen down and ran out of my room, down the back stairs, and out the kitchen door. Outside it was still raining like Niagara Falls, but I was so upset I barely noticed. I circled around the house and dashed past the police car. When I saw our bikes lying where we'd left them at the edge of the driveway, I breathed a sigh of relief.

With my hair dripping down around my face, I leaned over Marilyn's carrying case and clawed it open. Then I let out a long, loud moan. The china boy wasn't broken to bits. It was gone again. And it was all my fault.

15

Lugging my water-logged packages from P-town, I snuck back into the house like some kind of miserable wet rat. For the second time that afternoon I crept up the kitchen stairs so I wouldn't have to face anyone else. As I dripped and sloshed into my room, I made myself a solemn promise: I was going to go to Eunice and Brewster and tell them everything I knew, including how I'd stupidly recovered and relost their precious china boy. After my confession I was going to beg them to call the airlines and get me a ticket back to L.A. on the next possible flight.

Just then a knock sounded on my door. I opened it and stared at Bonnie's pale, worried face. Except for the fact that she wasn't dripping wet, she looked just about as miserable as I did. Until this trip, I reflected, I'd almost never seen an unhappy expression on Bonnie Bennington's face. But since we'd been at Bluff Point Dunes, I was getting more and more used to it.

My friend slumped into my room and threw herself down in my wicker rocker. I got right to the point. "Bonnie," I said, "I want to go home."

"So do I. But I just asked Grandmama, and she said that even though she's really sorry for everybody, she doesn't want us to go home until everything's been cleared up. Also, she thinks Sergeant Schott probably wouldn't let us leave anyway."

"Oh, that's just terrific," I snapped. "Especially when I don't have the smallest clue about what's going on!"

Bonnie sighed such a big sigh, it created a breeze through my wet hair. "I guess I'll have to tell you everything now," she said. "That is, everything *I* know. It's not much, but it's the least I can do to make up for the terrible time you're having here."

Hallelujah! I thought. The rest of the story. "I'm all ears," I said cornily.

"Okay. It goes back to last summer. Remember how I already told you we had a burglary, and Mopsy's pearls were stolen?"

I nodded up and down, showering the room with rainwater. "How could I forget that?" I asked. "Go on."

"Well there's something I didn't tell you. You see, Mopsy wore the pearls to dinner one evening, and the next morning she discovered they were gone, so at first we all assumed an intruder had broken in during the night and stolen them while we were asleep. That was scary enough. But then things got worse. We started doing some checking around the house, and we learned that was practically impossible!"

"What do you mean? What did you find out?"

"Well for one thing, there was no sign of any kind of forced entry. And for another, there were no footprints on the sandy path outside the house, *even though it had rained the evening before.*"

"Oh, dear," I said. "Then that means . . ."

"Right," said Bonnie. "That the burglar almost had to be someone from inside the house. Every one of us was a suspect—even Barry and Marilyn, who'd had the bad luck to be sleeping over that night because we were all going sailing early the next day."

"I see," I said slowly. "So then what? You all agreed to keep quiet about it because you didn't want to get each other in trouble?"

"Well not at first. Mopsy was really upset about the whole thing, as you might imagine. She kept *insisting* there had to have been a burglar and that we ought to call the police. She and Theo got into a big fight about it—in fact it's the only time I've ever heard the Kingsleys exchange a harsh word. Why, Mopsy called him an idiot!

Theo's feelings were hurt, but I can understand why she was so emotional. Her jewelry all belonged to her great-grandmother, and it's impossible to replace. And she just couldn't believe anyone in the cottage was a thief. And neither can I."

Neither could I. And I'd actually seen both Barry and Marilyn stealing things right out of the house! "What finally happened, Bonnie?" I asked. "How did you get through the rest of the summer?"

"Well Mopsy and Theo came up with some story to tell their insurance company, and I guess the company believed it. And after a while, we just stopped talking about the whole thing . . . except . . ."

"Except what?"

"Oh, well, of course, we were all pretty tense from then on. And," she paused and swallowed, "and it seemed like things started disappearing out of the house after that. I'm not sure about that though. I was probably imagining it."

"What kinds of things?" I asked. My inner voice was hinting that this could be significant.

"Oh, nothing important. Little things here and there. Like . . . oh, salt and pepper shakers and a cane and . . . oh, I don't know. I forget."

I wanted to keep on prying, but I had the sense I was losing my friend's attention. Bonnie has never been big on talking about depressing things for very long, and she had clearly reached her limit. All at once she smiled her famous smile. Like some kind of miracle eraser, it wiped her mental chalkboard clean. "And speaking of forgetting," she went on, "I haven't even told you why I'm really here. Grandmama sent me up to say the police have finished for today, and dinner will be served in about half an hour. It's going to be informal because Hettie's too upset about her interrogation to do any real cooking. Also Grandmama wants to remind us to get started on our costumes."

"Costumes! What costumes?"

"For the Fourth of July picnic tomorrow night," Bonnie said. "Didn't I tell you? Everybody wears costumes."

"No, you didn't tell me!" I said. "Anyway costumes are for Halloween, not Independence Day!"

"Really?" Bonnie looked thoughtful. "At Bluff Point Dunes we always wear costumes on the Fourth of July. I guess to an outsider it might seem a bit eccentric, but we do it every year because it's an old family custom."

"Well it's extremely original of you. But just where am I supposed to get a costume?"

"Oh, we'll go poke around up in the storage room in the attic behind Waldo and Hettie's apartment after dinner tonight," Bonnie said. "There's a lot of great stuff stored up there because there's more space here than in the Boston house. We can go through all the old trunks and try things on. It'll be fun!"

Ha! The last time she'd said that, I'd ended up coming to Cape Cod, and look how that was turning out! I couldn't believe Eunice wanted to go ahead and have a costume-party picnic with a thief actually living in the house! It seemed pretty typical of the Benningtons' policy of trying to have fun in the midst of crisis. It sounded crazy to me. But what else did I have to do?

"All right," I said. "Tomorrow night we'll go trick-or-treating in the sand. But now I need you to get out of here so I can go in and take a shower before dinner."

For the first time Bonnie noticed my wet hair and sodden clothes. "What happened to you anyway?" she asked.

I realized I hadn't told Bonnie anything about Barry and Marilyn and the china statuettes. I probably owed her an explanation now that she'd been honest with me, but I just didn't have the energy for all that talking. "It's a long story," I said. "I'll tell you later. For now let's just say I got caught in the rain."

She hauled herself up out of the creaky rocker. "All right, Kate," she said, "don't tell me why you were running around outside in the worst storm of the summer. But please do me a favor. Don't go snooping around trying to be some kind of Sherlock, Jr. There are just too many upsetting things going on." She gave a little wave and headed for her room. "I'll knock on your door at dinnertime."

When she was gone, I didn't waste a lot of time pondering what I'd just learned. I'd been surprised by what Bonnie had said, but not *that* surprised. Unsettling as it was, it made sense that the burglaries were an inside job. But I was too soggy to think about any of that right now. I was in desperate need of a long, hot shower.

Taking off my wet clothes felt like peeling the skin

off a grape. Why, I wondered on my way to the bathroom, why had not one, not two, but *three* people used some form of the word 'snoop' to describe me today? It just wasn't fair! I turned on the shower faucets full blast and climbed into the big old tub. Once again the strong, steamy spray went a long way toward soothing my troubled spirits. As I picked up my beloved thick cake of lavender soap, I reminded myself not to use so much of the perfumed lather this time. All at once a teasing little thought demanded my full attention.

Check it out! my inner voice ordered. I frowned and stuck the damp bar of soap right up against my nose. Yes, it did have a smell. Pleasant, lightly scented, just like the lavender sachet Grandma Irene keeps in her dresser drawers. But *nothing* like the heavy perfumey smell I'd noticed in my room yesterday afternoon!

What did it mean? I had no idea. It was probably a clue of some kind, but my mind was too exhausted to care. But at least one thing was sure. The soap did not make me smell like a branch of Perfume City Warehouse. And now I could lather up as many times as I wanted!

16

On the way down to dinner that night, Bonnie and I swore to a pledge. Under no circumstances would we bring up the mystery for the next twenty-four hours.

"The jewel thefts are in the hands of the police now, Kate," Bonnie told me, "and there's no point in worrying about them for our whole vacation. We're two simple school girls at the beach, and we're going to have fun whether we like it or not!"

I was so obsessed with the mystery that I wasn't sure I could keep to the pledge, but as usual, I was so swayed by the force of Bonnie's determined "Positive Thinking," that I agreed to give it a try. Soon I decided my merry-minded friend had had exactly the right idea. It *was* fun to think about things besides pearls, pilfering, and petty larceny. While the rest of the family and guests sat down to a cold supper in the main dining room, we decided we should eat roast beef, cheese, onion, and tomato submarine sandwiches piled up on Hettie's homemade rolls by ourselves in the children's dining room. Before long we were laughing and shrieking about nothing but L.A. stuff and people. Well that's not entirely true. Bonnie did mention that she thought Barry liked me, and I said, "Really?" about sixty times. But that was it for the local scene.

We even managed not to bring up Mopsy's missing bracelet or brooch or long lost pearls after dinner when we said hello and good-bye to everyone else and went up to the attic to unearth some picnic costumes. Actually that wasn't hard at all. Bonnie took me up a narrow set of attic steps that I hadn't even noticed before. Then we passed the door to Waldo and Hettie's apartment and went into a huge room that was absolutely stuffed with boxes and trunks. After that we got so interested in pawing through everything and trying on millions of outdated clothes, we really didn't think about anything else.

"Look at this!" I said after digging through an enormous black metal footlocker. I held up a wispy, white-and-purple gown that almost seemed to float up out of my hands. "This outfit absolutely *is* Mopsy!"

"Maybe so," Bonnie responded. "But she ought to wear this with it then." She showed me one of those fox stoles with the fox's real head still attached. "The expression on this creature's face looks exactly like Mopsy's when she's helping herself to seconds on dessert."

"But that thing has glass eyes!" I laughed.

"Well, Mopsy's eyes can be pretty glassy sometimes too," Bonnie began. "Whenever she's reaching for another . . . hey, wait a minute!" she interrupted herself. "This is perfect." She yanked an old ballgown and velvet cape out of a wooden crate and held it up under her chin. She was right. It was perfect. It would make her look just like a debutante, which wasn't particularly amazing since she would probably actually be one someday.

I kept digging and finally found a long, shiny black-and-white dress and cape that would make me look just like the Bride of Frankenstein. It was quite a bit too long, but Bonnie said we could fix that with a few safety pins.

"I'll do your face," she promised enthusiastically. "We'll put white glop all over you so you look really ghastly. Then we'll put some powder or something in your hair so you can have a white zig-zag streak up the front. With a little hair spray it'll be easy to get your hair to stand straight up on end."

"Thanks a lot, pal," I said with heavy irony. Of course I knew she was right. The tiniest bit of humidity makes my hair fuzz out like a Christmas tree with a permanent and, as you'll recall, there was more than a tiny bit of humidity hammering down on the roof over our heads.

We continued Bonnie's policy of forcing ourselves to have fun for the rest of the evening. There was no TV in the cottage, but there was a stereo in the living room, so we made popcorn (at last!), and asked Eunice if we could build a fire in the giant stone fireplace. With a slightly distracted air, she said she'd have Waldo do it for us, and I have to admit he did a beautiful job. He completely ignored me, of course, but when he was finished with the fire, he shuffled up to Bonnie and growled a good night that almost bordered on being pleasant. I was beginning to have a clearer idea about why Waldo detested me so much, and I wanted to ask Bonnie about it, but then I remembered we weren't talking about the mystery, so I bit my lip and kept quiet.

Anyway, with the cheerful fire flickering, the living room suddenly seemed a lot less like Dodger Stadium and a lot more like a real living room where two kids might snuggle up with a stack of magazines. We closed the big doors to the hall, put on a bunch of records, and stuffed ourselves with popcorn and some M&M's I'd bought in Provincetown. Every now and then, of course, the burglaries, etc., snuck back into my mind, but each time they did I shoved the thought away with another more important thought, like whether we needed to go back to the kitchen for more melted butter. I'm pretty sure Bonnie was doing the same kind of mental bull-dozing. Sometimes I'd see a kind of semi-worried expression flit across her face, and then right afterward she'd vigorously shake her head and concentrate on something else, like reading every single word on the back of an album cover.

At one point Eunice stuck her head in the door. "Just thought I'd check on you two lambs," she said with an exhausted Bennington smile. "Brewster and I are all in, and we're heading upstairs for the night." As she spoke, I remembered my decision to tell all to her and Brewster, but somehow I just couldn't bring myself to do it. For the first time since we'd arrived in Cape Cod, Eunice was finally starting to look like she might actually be some-body's grandmother, with tired lines around her eyes and sort of a saggy look around her mouth. I, for one, didn't want to be responsible for adding any more years to her appearance, at least not right now.

I'm not sure what the other adults were doing all this time, but whatever it was, they were quiet about it. When Bonnie and I finally went upstairs at midnight, the house was silent as a tomb, except of course for the sound of the rain and the ever-present boom of the surf outside. The two of us stayed in my room talking for a

while, and then crawled into our respective beds. I don't
know about Bonnie, but I slept like a dead person.

The next thing I knew, that powerful morning ocean
sun was beaming in through my windows and blasting
me in the face. But this time I didn't rise and shine along
with the light. I saw that the bedside clock said 6:30,
so I rolled over on my stomach and put my pillow over
my head.

"Kate! Wake up!"

Bonnie was tugging on my sleeve. With sleep-filled
eyes, I looked at my watch. Somehow it had gotten to
be three hours later. "Come on, Kate! Breakfast is ready.
Theo's already on thirds! Besides it's really hot outside.
Hurry up and eat so we can go swimming."

Well the rest of the day passed just the way I'd imagined days at Bluff Point Dunes passing when I'd said I'd
come along on this trip. After breakfast we put on swim-
suits and went down to the beach, which the rain had
washed till it was shiny clean. We spent the whole morning there, swimming, listening to the radio, playing
Frisbee, collecting shells, and yes, making sand castles.
Around 11:30 Barry and Marilyn strolled up in their
suits. They'd brought along a couple of little rubber rafts,
and Bonnie and Barry rode them in on the tops of the
waves like a couple of screaming, surfing cowboys. I sat
on the sand and talked to Marilyn, who shyly asked me
questions about growing up in a big city like Los Angeles.
She told me some stuff about her life in a small village,
and I was really fascinated. I mean, in some ways, such

as the size of our schools and towns, her world seemed to be the exact opposite of my own. But in other ways, such as our unreasonable teachers and bossy fathers, our lives seemed pretty much the same. She was so unthreatening and easy to talk to that by the end of the morning, I'd already started to think of her as a real friend—in spite of the fact that I'd seen her commit a crime only forty-eight hours before!

In fact Marilyn was so approachable, I was on the verge of asking her about what I was now thinking of as "The Mystery at Bluff Point Dunes." But before I worked up to it, Bonnie and Barry splashed over to join us on the sand. Bonnie suggested that we all walk back into the village together and have clam rolls at the clam bar there. Barry and Marilyn exchanged a quick glance. "Uh . . ." Barry began. "I'm not sure. . . ." But whatever he'd planned to say, he didn't get the chance to finish. In a brisk way that reminded me of Brewster, Bonnie had already charged up the wooden stairs to tell Eunice where we were going. The rest of us didn't have any choice but to follow.

As we hiked along the side of the road, the two other girls walked on ahead, and Barry and I trailed behind. Considering all the stuff we'd had to say to each other yesterday, we were now strangely silent. Finally we both started talking at once.

"What did you . . . ?" Barry said.

"What happened to the . . . ?" I said.

We stopped again and Barry gave his devilish grin and

said, "You first," so I said, "What happened to the china boy?"

The grin became a grimace. Barry skidded to a stop and grabbed my arm. "What do you mean what happened to it? You're the one who has it!"

"Had it, you mean!" I pulled my arm away. "Why do you always have to grab me whenever you ask me a question, anyway?"

"Sorry. It's getting to be a habit. But what do you mean about the china boy?"

"It disappeared out of Marilyn's carrying case sometime during the afternoon yesterday," I said. "And you were the only other person who knew it was in there!"

Barry directed his big brown eyes right at my gray ones. There was no sign of a twinkle or a wink. "You have to believe me, Kate," he said. "I don't know what happened to it. I didn't have anything to do with taking that statuette. Not this time, anyway."

Unbelievable, right? I mean it was pretty obvious to me that this kid could turn his earnest sincerity off and on like an automatic sprinkler system. But even so, call me a sucker if you want, for some insane reason I actually believed him again! This struck me as so stupid that I laughed out loud. "Now it's your turn to ask me a question," I said. "What do you want to know?"

"What you said when you were being grilled by the police, of course, dummy."

"Oh, well . . . I didn't tell them anything," I said. "I know it was wrong, and I'll probably go to jail for it. But that's what I did."

Now it was Barry's turn to laugh like a lunatic. I guess he was relieved because I hadn't sent him and Marilyn up the river. What a pair of hardened criminals we were turning out to be! If things kept going at this rate, the two of us would end up as the Bonnie and Clyde of our generation.

It didn't take long to get to the little village of Bluff Point Dunes, which was really just one main street with a post office, a general store, and a bunch of touristy little shops. Barry wanted to go right to the clam bar, and it goes without saying that I did too. But Bonnie had other ideas.

"Let's go say hi to your dad," she said to the twins. "I haven't even seen Uncle Gary yet this summer. And I know Kate would like poking around in the shop. Wait'll you see it, Kate. It's got everything from Mickey Mouse to Chippendale—and I'm not talking about the chipmunks."

It sounded like fun to me, but Barry and Marilyn both came up with about ninety excuses why we shouldn't go. "Dad's doing the books," Marilyn said in an unusually forceful voice. "He hates being disturbed."

"He's polishing some brass andirons," Barry said simultaneously. "We'd better not bother him."

I wondered how someone could do the books and polish brass at the same time, but I'm always happy to avoid meeting anyone's parent, so I once again turned my feet toward the clam bar. But Bonnie's face was wearing the politely stubborn expression I recognized from the cafeteria at school, when someone else tries to grab the last ice cream sandwich. "We won't *bother* him!" she said. "We'll just stick our heads in the door and say hello."

She started on another Brewster-like charge up the street, and the rest of us couldn't do anything but tag along behind again. But when we came to the little store named 'Williams Curiosity Shoppe,' we found a big Closed for Lunch sign hanging on the door.

Bonnie shrugged and Barry and Marilyn heaved twin sighs, but at that point I wasn't paying any attention to the three of them. My eyes were glued to the display in the shop window. A jumble of odds and ends, such as ancient porcelain baby dolls, brass door knockers, and old-fashioned jeweled fans, had been laid out around the outside edge of an antique cherry table. And right in the middle of the display, standing on a little pedestal, was a tiny china girl wearing a big droopy blue bonnet.

17

All during lunch I burned with anger. I'm sure the clam roll was good, but I was so mad, I barely tasted it. I ate it of course. To make matters worse, the whole time we were eating, Barry kept trying to catch my eye. I'm sure he was trying to send me a message with one of his winning winks, but this time I wasn't having any of it. I'd been dumb enough to believe him several times before.

But that was before Marilyn's stolen china girl had turned up in the middle of their own father's shop window with a *big* price tag on it! Of course I still didn't know where in the world the china *boy* was. But I did know I wouldn't believe a word Barry said anymore!

"You can fool a Clancy once," my dad likes to say. "But you have to get up pretty early in the morning to fool a Clancy twice!" Well despite Dad's witty words of wisdom, Barry Williams had just fooled a Clancy twice. I didn't plan to give him the chance to go for three.

After lunch the twins stayed in town to work on their costumes, and Bonnie said we'd see them tonight at the picnic. I didn't say a thing, not even good-bye. As we walked home, Bonnie shot me a couple of curious glances, but she didn't ask any questions. It was just as well because I couldn't have answered. I was still too mad to talk.

Back at the cottage everyone was already busy hauling out long tables and setting up lawn chairs for the picnic. As we came up to the house, we saw a woman in a gray suit climbing into a Buick with a World Life Property symbol on the door. A minute later we ran into Waldo, pruning some bushes and muttering something that sounded like "goll durned insurance companies." It didn't take Hercule Poirot to deduce that the lady in gray had been the Kingsleys' insurance company's investigator. There was no sign of Sergeant Schott or the other police officers anywhere, but I was positive we hadn't seen the last of them.

The next few hours were taken up with never-ending picnic preparations. I'd thought it was just a family affair, but apparently a lot of local people had been invited, as well as a group of Bennington relatives who were driving out from Boston. Even Great-Uncle Horace from Wellfleet (the one who'd cracked the raw egg on his head) was coming!

Hettie and Waldo were bustling back and forth around the place like a pair of hardworking ants storing up food for the winter. They hauled huge platters of shrimp on ice, dishes of caviar, plates full of cheese, gooseliver pate, smoked salmon and oysters, huge cut-glass bowls of melon and berries, and trays of French pastries. You name it, they hauled it. Eunice said she thought Bonnie and I might enjoy helping out, and soon we were both bustling back and forth too. Honestly, I was glad for the work. It took my mind off my bad mood, plus I always get a kick out of being around a lot of food. It sure wasn't like any picnic I'd ever seen before. In my family a picnic means a loaf of Wonder bread, a package of baloney, and if we're going fancy, a carton of potato salad from the deli counter at Ralph's.

Anyway I guess we must have worked harder than we thought, because Hettie came up to us at the end of the afternoon, wiped her big hands on her apron, and said, "Thanks for all the help, girls." Fortunately Bonnie was there to catch me before I keeled over from astonishment. I couldn't believe the woman was finally warming up to me, but her tone of voice had *almost* been pleasant. It was a miracle.

At about 6:30 P.M. Bonnie and I were just chowing down the last crumbs of our pre-party cheese and crackers snack when Sergeant Schott showed up at the front door. Brewster let him in and didn't seem very surprised to see him, which probably meant he'd known the policeman was coming. He glanced at the clock and then ordered Bonnie and me up to our rooms to work on our costumes.

By now, after all the hustling and bustling, I was getting pretty excited about the party, which just goes to show that I'm probably some kind of teenage manic-depressive, whose mood changes from good to bad and back again at the drop of a hat. Anyway, we put on our long dresses, and Bonnie pinned mine up so I wouldn't keep tripping over the skirt. Then she went to work on my makeup. She'd found some kind of white cream somewhere, and she glopped it all over my face till my skin was the exact same shade as a recent vampire victim's. Then she globbed on a ton of green eye shadow and mascara so my eyes would have that special haunted look.

After that she tackled my hair. Just as she'd predicted, it only took a few spritzes of hair spray (she said she'd liberated a can of Mopsy's from the room next door, but I guessed the stuff was really for Theo's toupee) along with several hundred bobby pins to make my fuzzy locks stand up just like the real Bride's. When the two of us studied our reflections in the mirror in my room, I wondered if maybe I'd let Bonnie go just a little too far. I mean I looked so scary, it was *scary*!

Bonnie, on the other hand, looked like something out of a 1940's issue of *Cosmopolitan*. She'd parted her hair on the side and given herself a big red lipstick mouth like they always have in the movies. With the old-fashioned—but flattering—dress and cape, I could just imagine her going ballroom dancing with a World War II aviator at the Copacabana, or wherever they went way back then.

By the time we came downstairs some guests' cars were already pulling into the driveway. Almost everyone was wearing a costume. Eunice was dressed like a maiden out of a fairy tale, so naturally Brewster was clanking around—as fast and efficiently as ever—in a suit of armor. Mopsy Kingsley was wearing one of her never-ending supply of big-sleeved, wispy flowing gowns, and Theo had on an ancient threadbare tuxedo. Mopsy came over and told us we looked "simply lovely" (which I didn't quite know how to take, given my costume) and said the party reminded her of the grand parties her family used to have when she was a young girl. She clasped our hands in hers, and I felt at least four heavily jeweled rings on her fingers. "You have to admire Mopsy's guts," I whispered to Bonnie. "Wearing all those rocks with a burglar on the loose!"

"She probably feels they're safer if she's wearing them," Bonnie whispered back. "Hi, Hettie. Hello, Waldo."

The housekeeper and gardener had also changed clothes for the occasion. Hettie wore a black maid's uniform with a little white apron, and Waldo wore a brown suit and a tie. The suit didn't fit him very well, but it was a lot better than the stained overalls he usually skulked around in. When he saw beautiful Bonnie come into the room, he gave his bizarre impression of a smile and growled, "Well, Hettie, look how our little Bonnet is growing up into a lady." At least I think that's what he said. Anyway if I'd heard him right, it was the nicest, most normal thing I'd ever heard him say.

Then the party really began in earnest. The evening was pretty warm, so everyone just stayed outside after they arrived, and ate and talked and ate some more. I'd been wondering how people would manage with their costumes on the sand, but most of the action was up on the grassy lawn in front of the house, so it wasn't a problem. At about 8:00 P.M. I saw Marilyn and Barry arrive with a brown-haired man who had to be their father because he looked just like them. The twins were dressed like hoboes, but their father was wearing plain old every-day clothes, which made me remember what Barry had told me about his father's feud with the Benningtons. I supposed his lack of costume was some kind of anti-Bennington statement.

As time went by, I kept expecting Barry to come over and try to talk to me again, and I was all geared up to ignore him when he did. Instead, though, he lounged over to the gazebo and sat down with a bunch of noisy laughing town kids who were dressed like rock stars. He was so cool he didn't so much as glance in my direction. Even though I never wanted to speak to him again, this made me feel like crying, which I couldn't afford to do because I had sixteen tons of mascara on my eyes, and it would have been a total face disaster.

Anyway Bonnie and I spent most of the time wandering

around avoiding her relatives and gaping at all the amazing costumes. People had really outdone themselves. There were the usual vampires and witches and Frankensteins of course. And because it was the Fourth of July, there were three Statues of Liberty and even a pair of American flags. All the creatures and objects seemed to be having a good time. Mopsy and Theo were talking to a bunch of their acquaintances from Beacon Hill, and Brewster was competently clanking around in his armor making sure everyone had enough to eat and drink.

It began getting dark around 9:00 P.M., and Waldo and some of the Boston uncles started lugging big cartons down the stairs to the beach. Bonnie told me that all the people who lived along the beach always tried to outdo each other's fireworks displays every year, so I should be ready for a really big show. "Come on," she said, pulling on my arm. "Let's go inside. The best view is from one of the upstairs balconies."

We started toward the deserted house, but just as we reached the front door, someone called Bonnie's name. She looked back, and I heard her groan under her breath. "Oh, hi, Great-Uncle Horace," she said.

A little old man in a Paul Revere costume teetered toward us, and immediately launched into a long story about his hobby, which apparently had something to do with tracking down every single Bennington living or dead in the whole wide world. "This could go on all night," Bonnie muttered in my ear while she smiled politely at her uncle. "Save yourself! Go on inside. As soon as I can escape, I'll meet you on the balcony."

I silently slipped into the shadows and made my way into the empty house. Even though people had been carrying things inside and outside all evening, some thrifty soul had carefully turned off all the lights, and except for a few silvery moonbeams, the place was almost completely dark. As I went through the front hall toward the stairs, I caught a blurry glimpse of my reflection in the hall mirror, and just about screeched out loud. In the pale light I really did look ghastly. I pitied anyone who ran into *me* at the end of a long hallway.

Upstairs the house was even darker than below. I ran my fingers over the walls in search of a light switch, but I couldn't find one. Fortunately I knew the way to my room pretty well. I spotted my door and reached out to turn the knob. But as I touched it, it moved all by itself! As I snatched my hand away and stared in rigid, heart-stopping fear, the knob turned slowly to the right. Then my door began opening inward.

Suddenly I came to my senses. I threw myself back against the wall and sidled away as fast as I could, like some kind of horrified human hermit crab. My plan was to reach Bonnie's room and scuttle inside before I was discovered by the intruder. But before I got to her door, a figure stepped out of my room into the hall.

This is it, I thought. The game's up. But luckily for me, I was wrong. The shadowy figure didn't even turn in my direction. After closing my door, the intruder walked straight across the hall and down the stairs. A second later I heard the front door *crreak* open and *crreak* closed. Of course the creaking door wasn't the only telltale sound my horrified ears had to listen to. The other sound was the quick, clamorous clanking of a clunky suit of armor.

18

"Good grief!" I said out loud. "Brewster is the thief!" But as soon as I said these words, I knew they couldn't be true. Brewster Bennington was rich, wasn't he? Why did he need to steal anything from anybody? And besides, even if he was the thief, why would he have been in *my* room of all places? A jewel thief would have better luck in the broom closet!

"No, no, no," I muttered to myself. "Brewster can't be the thief." Of course I knew in my heart this hadn't exactly been proven beyond a shadow of a doubt. I suppose weirder things have turned out to be true. And there was no denying he had just been lurking around in my room. I opened my door and went in to investigate. I searched for the light switch, but was interrupted before I found it. BOOM! Loud shots cracked through the air. *Kah-Boom!* Red, green, and gold lights showered through the night outside my window.

AhhhHHHHHHhhhh. I love fireworks with a passion. In two seconds flat I forgot all about being a detective and ran toward the balcony for a better look. But before

I got there I heard crack, crack, *cracketty-cracketty, Blam!* One strong, solid, bright, white ball lit up the sky. And out of the corner of my eye, I saw something shiny and gold glinting on my pillow.

The bright white ball outside faded, but not before I'd grabbed up the object on my bed. Anyway I didn't need any light to know what it was. My missing gold locket, mysteriously returned from . . . from where? Without really thinking, I put the locket on. It didn't exactly match my Bride of Frankenstein costume, but I figured my neck was the safest place to keep it.

My mind was fizzing and sizzling like the fireworks over the ocean, and I sat down on the edge of my bed to try to calm down. Be rational! I ordered myself. What is one thing we are almost positively sure about? I thought for a minute. *Well*, I answered slowly, *Brewster has to be the one who returned my locket since he was just in here. And he's a sure bet to be the one who returned my watch because he was the one I spotted through Barry's binoculars yesterday.* But how had he gotten my jewelry in the first place, and why had he been so sneaky about giving it back? It didn't make sense. Unless. Unless he was protecting someone. And whom would Brewster be apt to be protecting . . . ?

For some reason the image came to me of my mother's dear departed Aunt Frieda. I'd always loved Aunt Frieda because she'd given me unlimited peanut M&M's whenever we visited her. But I'd also known she had a problem because I'd overheard my parents talking about her one night. Apparently Aunt Frieda couldn't stop herself from taking things that belonged to other people. But why was I thinking about her *now*? Oh my gosh! A major Miss Marplesque detective theory materialized in my mind, and I did some quick remembering and calculating of opportunities and means. With my mental computer working at top speed, I got to my feet and hurried out of my room. This time I was actually going to earn the nickname of Snoopy.

As I quickly crept along the hallway, I ticked off a list on my fingers. One: My new theory explained Waldo's and Hettie's dislike of outside visitors. Two: It explained the disappearance and reappearance of my watch and locket. Three: If I was right, there was one person who'd always "happened" to be poking around in the right place at the right time, right before something had mysteriously disappeared.

I came to Brewster and Eunice's room, stepped inside, and reached for the light switch. Then I changed my mind. Like my own room, this one faced the ocean, where the crowd of picnickers was gathered. Someone down there would be sure to notice a light on the second floor and just might come in to investigate. That was the last thing I wanted.

Actually I could see fairly well without the lamp. Moonlight beamed in through the window, along with the off-again-on-again sparkles from the fireworks, and I took a good look around. The Benningtons' room was similar to my own, though larger and with two sets of end tables, bureaus, chairs, and so on. On tiptoe I started

Sherlock Holmesing around the room. As I lurked and skulked in and out between the furniture, my guilty conscience hurled insults at me, and I had to keep reminding it that I wasn't trying to hurt anyone. In fact, if I was right, I could solve the mystery without my prime suspect's having to get in trouble—or much trouble anyway. At least Aunt Frieda never had. Everyone had just understood that she had a problem.

I started my serious snooping with the nearest bureau, which, from the perfume bottles and silver brush and mirror, looked like it had to belong to Eunice. I pawed through the clutter on top and then opened the top drawer. Inside I discovered a pile of Liberty of London silk scarves and some scented soap. I was about to close the drawer and move on to the next when I caught sight of a small metal box almost buried by the scarves. I dug it out and pulled off the top. Then I thrust the box under the light of the nearest moonbeam.

Ka-Boom! My long sigh was lost in the *blam* of another window-rattling firecracker, but I was so rattled myself, I barely noticed the noise. I mean, when I'd started this searching business I'd thought it was a long shot. I hadn't really believed I'd find anything important, especially not this fast. But I had. I'd found what almost had to be Theo Kingsley's missing abalone tie clip. And I'd also found my old friend, the china boy statuette.

Get out of here! my inner voice screamed at me. *Now!* But I didn't have the chance to move because in that instant, two powerful, stumpy hands closed around my neck. I tried to scream, but I couldn't because you need breath to scream, and mine was choked off. I wasn't sure if I was seeing stars or just fireworks, but it didn't matter. Either way I was still just as terrified.

"I knew you spelled trouble," a voice growled in my ear, "the minute I laid eyes on you!"

Suddenly someone snapped on the overhead light. "Waldo! Please let go at once!" Brewster's normally smooth and cultured voice was close to a bark.

Waldo loosened his hold, but only slightly. "I caught her red-handed," he said. "Snooping around in your room. Tryin' to get people in trouble."

"I can understand why you're upset, Waldo," Brewster said. "And I'm as shocked as you are. But I'm sure Kate will have an explanation. So why don't you go back downstairs for now and help Hettie with the picnic? I'll come and speak to the two of you later."

The hands let go of my neck, and heavy footsteps lumbered out of the room. Only after I was absolutely positive Waldo was gone, did I recover enough control over my shaking body to make it turn around and face Brewster, who was still wearing his suit of armor, except for the headpiece. With a start of surprise, I saw he wasn't alone. Marilyn Williams, looking wide-eyed and bewildered in her hobo outfit, was standing right next to her grandfather.

"I . . . I'm sorry," I stammered. "I know it looks like I'm some kind of burglar, but I'm not. I was just in here . . ."

"Snooping?" Brewster supplied in his brisk way.

"Right," I said miserably. "Snooping. I have a good reason. But I don't suppose you believe that."

"As a matter of fact, my dear, I do. And from what my granddaughter here tells me, you're not the only one who's been engaging in this type of well-intentioned activity."

Marilyn and I exchanged glances, and she gave me a tiny, almost imperceptible wink. I'll be eternally grateful for that one small signal that I wasn't entirely alone in this mess.

Brewster clanked around the room for a minute, as if trying to figure out what to do with us. Then he sat down in one of the rocking chairs, put the tips of his fingers together, and cleared his throat. "Ahem." I could imagine him opening up a board meeting in much the same manner.

"I think a few explanations are in order here," he said. "Why don't you begin, Kate, by telling us why you were seized by a notion to come up here and go through Eunice's belongings?"

"Well," I said, "I had an idea a while ago . . . I know it sounds pretty wild . . . but you see, I had an Aunt Frieda who used to . . ."

"Get to the point, dear girl!" Brewster commanded.

"Yes, sir. With all the strange things that have been going on, I was wondering . . . could Mrs. Bennington be some kind of kleptomaniac or something? I mean I just happened to notice that she was the one person who was always around right before something disappeared, and . . ."

As my voice trailed off, the fireworks boomed and *bammed* their heads off outside. I'd been anticipating some kind of wild outburst or denial from Brewster or Marilyn, but inside the room the silence grew and spread like a monstrous mudslide on the Pacific Coast Highway. I cleared my throat and went on. "I thought that's why you returned my locket and my watch to my room without saying anything to anyone, Mr. Bennington."

Brewster reacted with another "ahem," but Marilyn didn't make a peep. Bravely I plodded on. "I figured it had to be Mrs. Bennington," I said, "partly because she always had the opportunity to take the things, but also because she's so nice, she inspires so much loyalty in people, and everyone seemed so busy scurrying around trying to protect someone. And then just now, well, I found these things in Eunice's drawer." I opened my sweaty little palm and held out the tie clip and the china boy.

Brewster reached over and took the tie clip and statuette out of my hand. "Theo's clip," he said. "I recognize it. And this statuette is a very nice piece of work. Who does it belong to?" My mouth opened wide in surprise. Brewster sounded as if he'd never seen the little china boy before! But I'd seen it with my own eyes right downstairs in the Benningtons' living room.

Marilyn's quiet voice provided the explanation. "It's my father's," she said. "He bought that one and a matching little girl at an auction last month. He was going to put them up for sale at the shop. But the other day when we came for tea, I saw the two of them in the living room of this house! So I . . ."

"You made much the same assumption as our friend, Kate, here," Brewster interrupted. "Based on past events, you'd also concluded your grandmother was a klepto-maniac. So you assumed she had taken the figures from the shop and brought them here for herself."

"Right," Marilyn said. "Ever since last summer, it seems like things have been disappearing whenever Grandma's been in the vicinity. Mostly it was just little things that didn't matter, but what with so much of Mopsy's jewelry being stolen, we were afraid Grandma might get in trouble with the police. We thought it would just be easier all the way around if we could replace the china boy and girl without Dad's ever having to find out she'd taken them. After all, we didn't want his re-lationship with Grandma to get any worse than it already is."

"Your father is much too intelligent and enlightened a person to take an attitude like that, young lady!" Brew-ster said sternly. "Kleptomaniacs are not criminals, but rather people afflicted with a most unfortunate malady. I'm positive your father would be most under-standing and compassionate if your grandmother had the bad luck to suffer from kleptomania. But that is neither here nor there because I can assure you that she does *not* suffer from it. She has never taken anything from your father's shop, nor from anyplace else. You will be wise to believe me, because I know it for a fact."

He turned to me and continued his lecture. "And as for your locket and watch, Kate," he said, "you are correct about one thing. I did find them here, on two different occasions, mixed in among Eunice's things. But unlike everyone else who chose to sneak around behind our backs, I went straight to Eunice and asked her if she knew what the items were doing here. She was as puzzled and concerned as I, and we put our heads together to try to come up with an explanation. We failed in that effort, but decided the best course was to return your belongings to your room as you would undoubtedly be happy to have them back."

There was another mudslide of a silence while we all tried to sort out our confused thoughts. "So what actually is the story here?" I asked myself out loud. "On the one hand, we have things disappearing all over the place. And on the other hand, we have *most* of the things showing up again in fairly obvious places in this house. Then we have everyone," I glanced at Brewster's stern face, "that is *almost* everyone suspecting that Eunice is a kleptomaniac. It's almost as if . . ." My voice trailed off, and I became lost in thought.

"But Gramps," Marilyn said in her soft voice. "If Grandma isn't a kleptomaniac, then what in the world is happening around here?"

Brewster's aristocratic face looked angry and determined. "I'm not certain, Marilyn," he said. "But I do know this. I will not rest until I get to the bottom of it!"

19

Well, after that statement there didn't seem to be a lot more the three of us could talk about. Marilyn asked if she could have the china boy back so she could return it to the shop the next day. Brewster wanted to rejoin the party, and suddenly so did I. I believe I had some idea about accidentally bumping into Barry and telling him I was sorry for thinking he was a thief (again). If, that is, I could work up the courage to swallow my pride along with my gooseliver pate.

Anyway the three of us left Eunice and Brewster's room, went down the stairs, walked out of the house, and went our separate ways. Brewster hurried away to find Eunice (I prayed he wouldn't tell her what he'd found me doing), and Marilyn went off in search of her father. I passed one of the food tables and grabbed up a chocolate eclair from a dessert tray. Greedily devouring the dynamite combination of chocolate, custard, and flaky pastry, I started wandering through the crowd, pretending I wasn't looking for Barry.

But I didn't have much luck with my non-search. I

spotted the group of rock star town kids, but Barry wasn't entertaining them anymore. Then I saw Marilyn and Mr. Williams standing by themselves, drinking punch and quietly talking. But no Barry.

Finally I started walking in a giant ring around the entire party, like a tiger circling her prey. As I walked, I tried to make sense of what I'd just learned inside. From what Bonnie had told me, things had been disappearing from around the house beginning with Mopsy's pearls last summer. Mopsy still clung to the idea of an outside intruder, but from the pattern of events, Marilyn, Barry, and I had all deduced that Eunice was a kleptomaniac. Come to think of it, Waldo and Hettie had probably had the same idea. It was the best explanation for their absurd hostility toward outsiders in the house. Was it just a coincidence that we'd all come up with this wrongheaded (if you believed Brewster, which I did) conclusion? It didn't seem very likely.

I might have worked the whole thing out right then and there and saved myself a lot of grief, but in that instant I caught sight of Great-Uncle Horace tottering around in his Paul Revere outfit. "Oh, no!" I cried through my last mouthful of eclair. *"Bonnie!"* I'd completely forgotten my promise to meet my friend on the balcony in my room, and she'd probably been standing up there for an eternity.

I wiped the dessert off my face and some of my monster lipstick came off on my hand. As I hurried across the lawn, I must have kicked out one of my safety pins, because I almost tripped over the hem of my dress. When I reached the house, I peered up at my balcony, trying to locate Bonnie, but it was too shadowy to see a thing. I called her name a few times and got no response. She must have given up on me, I decided.

But I still had to go inside and make sure she wasn't standing around up there, waiting and waiting. I went to the front door and paused. The vague half-baked theories in the back of my mind made me feel a reluctance, almost a foreboding, about going back in. I shook myself and tried to stop being so silly. I'd just run up the stairs, shout for Bonnie, and run right back down.

As I stepped inside, all the lights suddenly went off, and I stopped in my tracks. I felt along the wall for the light switch, but when I flipped it, nothing happened. Terrific, I thought. All we need right now is a power failure. For the second time that night, I walked across the dark hall toward the stairs. *Blam!* Clatter, clatter, clatter. Can you believe it? I'd just crashed into my old friend, the brass urn filled with antique canes! For some reason I bent over, picked up the nearest cane, and carried it up the stairs with me. I couldn't explain this continuing feeling of impending doom, but having a weapon made me feel a little less nervous about prowling around in this big, dark house.

I reached my room with no problem this time, and once again, flipping the light switch brought no results. When I looked out on the balcony, there was no sign of Bonnie. Oh, well, I thought. She probably got tired of waiting and went back outside. Anyway the fireworks show was almost finished, so there was really no point in staying up here. Great! I could kiss this place good-bye.

Still clutching the heavy cane, I started for the door, when a sudden thought stopped me. Had Bonnie told me to meet her on my balcony or on *her* balcony? I tried to remember, but I just couldn't. It's not that surprising really—so many confusing and upsetting things had been happening, my brain batteries had just about lost their charge.

I decided to cut through the bathroom and dash through Bonnie's room, just to be sure. A quick check told me she wasn't there, or on her balcony either. All right, Clancy! I said to myself. You've done your duty. Now get out of this spooky house and go back outside where there are lights and people—and second helpings on eclairs!

I was more than happy to follow my own orders. But as I crossed Bonnie's room on my way to the hall door, I couldn't help noticing a slightly open door on her far wall. I'd seen the door before when I'd been in there, but I'd always assumed it was an extra closet. Now, though, the door was open just enough to tell me that it really led into someone else's bedroom.

I knew I shouldn't go in. I'd already done my quota of snooping for the night. But something—could it be my nose? was it actually twitching?—was drawing me closer and closer to that room. Before I knew it I was using my cane to push the door the rest of the way open.

Then there I was, standing in the middle of the strange bedroom.

It looked pretty much like all the other bedrooms I'd seen in the house. White wicker rocker, bureaus, beds, window facing the ocean, the usual stuff. But something about the place was bothering me, trying to send me a secret message. *Snnnnifffff!* What *was* the problem with my nose?

I wandered closer to the nearest bureau, and my eyes grew wide. My mom would have been astonished. The assortment of clutter made my dresser at home look neat! There were scarves, books, hairbrushes, scissors, nail files, tweezers, jewelry boxes (jewelry boxes? significant, significant!), perfume, and cologne bottles. . . . *Ah-Choo!*

Say that last one again, Clancy! my nose commanded.

Wha . . . ? You mean, perfume and cologne bottles? *Right!*

Oh my gosh! You mean the flowery smell! It *is* in here, isn't it?

That's what I've been trying to tell you.

I grabbed up the nearest bottle and pulled out the stopper. No, that wasn't the one. But I kept on sniffing, and finally I found it. Smashed right up next to the nostrils, the smell was enough to make you keel over. In the pale light from the window, I squinted at the label. "Sultan of Spice," I read. "Sensual cologne for the man's man."

I sat down on the rocker and giggled out loud. 'Man's man,' indeed. Give me a break!

Get serious, Clancy! my inner voice shouted. *And get out of here! Don't you realize . . . ?*

Unfortunately my inner warning came just a few seconds too late. The door to the hall opened, and a man walked into the room. In the dark I couldn't see his face, but his shadowy shape immediately told me who he was. The shadows also told me he wasn't alone. He was holding on to a companion. As the pair moved into the room, a thin slice of moonlight fell for just an instant on a pale, shiny lock of blond hair. Oh, *no!* My friend Bonnie had been taken prisoner.

20

If I do say so myself, I acted fast. I was positive the newcomers hadn't seen me sitting motionless in the dark. So, I thought, if I could silently slide off the chair, soundlessly slither across the floor, and stealthily slip under the bed, I might be able to hide until there was a chance to escape and go for help.

"The best laid plans . . . ," my mom likes to say. I'm not sure exactly what this means, but I know Mom always says it when something has just gotten screwed up. And she certainly would have said it now. As I started my silent slide off the chair, my toe got stuck in the hem of my long dress, and I pitched forward and landed smack on my face. *Wham!* The crash was tremendous.

The figures froze. Then the larger one snapped on a flashlight. Two sets of startled eyes stared down at me. "Hello, Mr. Kingsley," I said from my position on the floor. "Hi, Bonnie."

"Run, Kate!" Bonnie cried. "Go get help!"

Theo's round face reddened, and his eyes bugged with anxiety. "Oh, lordy," he said. "Two of you now. What a muddle. Have to ask you young ladies for a bit of peace and quiet. Have to work out a plan, don't you know."

"I'll be quiet," I promised. "But if you don't stop pulling on Bonnie like that, I'll scream my head off!" As I spoke, my nostrils pointed out that almost every time I'd noticed the flowery smell, Theo had shown up almost immediately afterward. In other words I'd had the solution to this whole mystery right in the palm of my hand—or nose—since the very beginning. If only I'd paid more attention to my own senses!

But there was no time for regrets. Right now Theo was looking like he wished I were on Neptune, but at least he had loosened his hold on my friend's arm. He kept his other hand deep inside the pocket of his shiny old tuxedo.

"Kate," Bonnie said in a slightly hysterical rush of words, "I don't understand this. When I went into my room to meet you before, *he* . . ." She twisted her neck to look at Theo, "*he* was already in there, poking around in the dark. I saw him take some of my stuff, and then

127

all at once he saw me and went nuts. He grabbed me and said I had to stay with him because he had a gun in his pocket! But it doesn't make any sense because all I saw him take out of my drawer were some cheap plastic beads and earrings. So why . . . ?"

"He was going to plant them around the cottage," I interrupted. "To make everyone think your grandmother Eunice was a kleptomaniac. And he wants everyone to think that because . . . because . . ." I paused to sort out my thoughts, and the answer suddenly jumped into my mind. "Because *he* really *is* a real thief. No one suspected him because he was stealing from his own wife. And why is he stealing from his own wife? Why? Why? Why . . . it's for the insurance! That's it! He steals the stuff and maybe even sells it somewhere. And then there's the insurance policy on top of it. I bet that's what he was checking up on in Provincetown that day Barry and I saw him. There was an office of that insurance company right there on the block with the cookie shop!"

"Insurance," Bonnie repeated. She stared at me as if I'd completely lost my mind. "That doesn't make any sense. I don't have insurance on my plastic jewelry, Kate, and even if I did, how could Theo benefit from that?"

Bonnie's sweet and sunny, and I love her dearly, but she's not always what you'd call quick on the uptake. But I didn't get the chance for further explanations because Theo interrupted our conversation. "Please! Be quiet. Last thing we need is a crowd up here." He went over and closed the curtains and then snapped on a bedside lamp. The light didn't come on of course, because the power was still off, probably because Theo himself had thrown the circuits in the basement before he started pilfering Bonnie's plastic jewelry. He muttered and then propped his flashlight on top of the lamp so he wouldn't have to carry it around with him. As he moved back and forth across the thin beam of light, I studied the features of his round face. The man didn't look anything like the chubby, friendly, noisy person I'd come to know in the past few days. Now he looked worried, scared, tired, and dangerously desperate. It was clear that we'd badly messed up his plans. He was wondering if he could avoid being caught, publicly humiliated, and probably sent to jail. And he was trying to figure out what on earth he should do with Bonnie and me.

Bonnie inched her way toward me. As she moved, she glanced over her shoulder in Theo's direction, but he barely seemed to notice what she was doing. I guess he figured we couldn't get past him to the door, so he didn't have to worry about us for the time being.

My friend reached the wicker rocker and sat down in it. "What did you mean about the insurance on my stuff?" she whispered, leaning down toward me.

"Not the insurance on *your* stuff!" I answered impatiently. "The insurance on Mopsy's stuff! Don't you see? Lots of things have been stolen around here. But just about the only really *valuable* things were Mopsy's bracelet and brooch, which were heavily insured! So if Theo took the stuff from his own wife . . ."

"He could have us all believing that Grandmama had stolen the jewelry along with everything else, while he was cashing in on the insurance money. So that's why things have been disappearing all over the place. That's just terrible!"

As Bonnie got angrier and angrier, her voice got louder and louder, and finally Theo seemed to notice she was just about screaming. He got up off the bed and came over in our direction. The ends of his handlebar mustache created huge threatening shadows on his jowly cheeks. "Quiet down!" he barked. His jolly gentlemanly manner had almost completely disappeared. But I noticed that he'd taken his hand out of his tuxedo pocket. The shiny black fabric lay as flat as a pancake against his side. I was positive Theo's gun had been nothing but a bluff to scare Bonnie.

A sudden inspiration came to me, and my fingers started scrabbling around on the floor near the rocker. Bingo, I found what I wanted. "So who's going to make us be quiet, Theo?" I taunted loudly.

Pretty brave, right? But I had to do something. It seemed to me that in his frightened, nervous condition it would be easy to provoke Theo into doing something foolish. And was I ever right! At the sound of my noisy bellowing voice, the man simply snapped his twig. He grunted like some kind of wounded water buffalo and then reached out his hand to cover my mouth. Just as he was about to make contact with my face, I lashed out with my heavy cane. It struck him smack on both shins, and he yowled and pitched forward. Unfortunately he landed right on top of me, pinning me to the floor.

"Run, Bonnie!" I yelled, struggling to escape. "Go get help!" My friend didn't waste a second. She leapt up out of the rocker and flew toward the hall door. I would have been right behind her except that my long dress got all tangled up around my legs and I couldn't get out from under Theo's heavy weight. But anyway it didn't make much difference. Just as Bonnie reached the door, someone else opened it.

In her flowing, wispy gown, Mopsy Kingsley fairly floated into the room. As she made a survey of the wild scene, her vague blue eyes grew wide and then suddenly seemed to snap into focus. It must have looked pretty bizarre, all right, what with the weird light from the propped-up flashlight, me in my Bride outfit lying scrunched up under huffing, puffing Theo, and Bonnie in her debutante ensemble panting by the door.

"Mopsy!" Bonnie gasped. "Thank heaven you're here. You have to help us. But . . . I'm sorry to say there's bad news. We know who's been stealing your jewels!"

"Do you really, dear?" Mopsy asked. Her voice was as whispery and sweet as ever. And remarkably calm. *Uh-oh*, said my inner voice.

But the ever-optimistic Bonnie didn't notice a thing. "Yes," she rushed on. "And I'm afraid it's . . . it's Theo, your husband. He's been stealing your jewelry for the insurance."

"But this is just dreadful, dear." Mopsy put a hand

on Bonnie's arm and gently pushed her all the way back into the bedroom. My friend looked puzzled and then astonished, but after my initial shock and dismay, I realized it all made sense. Endearing, grandmotherly Mopsy *had* to be in on the scheme. It's the only way their plan could have worked.

With a lot more grunting and groaning, Theo finally managed to haul himself back up to his feet. "Well, Theo dear, I see you've had your usual problems with the arrangements this evening," Mopsy said.

"They surprised me, pet, don't you know," he said apologetically. "One of them found me in her room. Had to pretend I had a gun in my pocket. But now the one on the floor smacked me with something. Problem is, what's to be done with them?"

His wife looked at Bonnie and me and gave us her quaint, Auntie Mopsy smile. Was I imagining things, or had her face always had that disturbingly demented quality? I thought maybe it had, particularly when she'd been talking about how she'd always been jealous of her dear, dear friend Eunice. I'd just been too absorbed in other things to notice.

"I'm so sorry you two girls had to get caught up in this dreadfully tacky business," Mopsy was saying as sweetly as ever. "None of it was supposed to happen like this. We realized last summer that we simply had to have more money. Things are so expensive nowadays, and . . . well, you must understand that we just could not go on like that!"

"So you then decided to steal your own jewelry?" I

prompted. Maybe if I could keep her talking, someone would come by and help us.

"Yes, of course, dear," Mopsy responded distractedly. "And believe me, no one but the insurance company was supposed to be involved. But after our first burglary last summer, absolutely everything imaginable started to go wrong! Theo was supposed to fake a break-in from the outside, but the dunderhead had the notion that *I* was doing it, so he didn't do a thing! I truly became *hysterical* the next day when everyone realized the burglar had to be someone from inside the house."

"So in order to divert suspicion from yourselves," I said, "you created the kleptomania cover-up?"

"Exactly, my dear," Mopsy said. "We arranged things so people would think beloved, *beautiful* Eunice was going about pocketing possessions, and just look what happened! Everyone tripped over their own toes trying to shield the poor thing from the police investigation."

Hmmm. Now that I thought about it, Mopsy always complimented her old friend in a way that made Eunice sound just a bit too nauseatingly perfect. I should have noticed that before too.

"At any rate," Mopsy went on, "no one even thought of investigating *us*. We were really quite safe. Until tonight that is." As she spoke, Mopsy dreamily drifted across the room toward her bureau. When she got to it, she pulled open the top drawer. She reached inside. When her hand came back out, it was holding an ugly dangerous-looking little gun! Double *ulp*.

I wanted to get close to Bonnie so we could make some

kind of plan. But she was still shaking in her slippers over near the doorway, and I was still twisted up in my ridiculous position on the floor by the rocker. If only we could get rid of the flashlight, somehow, at least one of us might be able to escape in the darkness.

That gave me an idea. Although Theo was busily rubbing his shins where I'd hit him, he seemed to have forgotten all about my trusty old cane. In the beam from the flashlight, I could just see it, sticking halfway out from where it had rolled under the bed. If I could just grab it one more time, I might be able to knock the flashlight off the top of the lamp.

Suddenly I made my move. Screeching "Run, Bonnie, run!" I threw myself stomach-down across the floor. I grabbed the cane and hurled it at the flashlight. Unfortunately I missed by a mile. The cane bounced onto the top of the bed and came to rest on the pillow. But I had accomplished something. I'd created enough of a diversion for Bonnie to yank open the door and run out into the hall.

For a few seconds I was so astonished by my own bravery that I couldn't move. Suddenly it dawned on me that I hadn't been shot and that no one was sitting on me. I scrambled to my feet just in time to see Theo's rotund shape disappear out the hall door as he ran after Bonnie.

Were they both really gone? Was I really free? I started toward the hallway, but just as I reached it, a soft shadow flowed out from behind the door. Mopsy! I tried to run, but a large, well-padded hand took hold of my arm.

"Poor Theo probably won't catch Bonnie," Mopsy said. "But you might be able to help me get away, dear. You and I can walk out of this room and go down the kitchen stairway. If we meet anyone, we can simply speak in our normal way, and no one will suspect a thing."

She was talking as if we were a couple of girlfriends planning to sneak out of the house without telling our parents. But I hadn't forgotten she still had that little gun tucked up inside the flowing sleeve of her gown. Unlike Theo's, her gun really existed. It was hard to believe plump, huggable Mopsy would actually shoot me. But it was also hard to believe she'd masterminded a complex scheme for covering up an insurance fraud scam—and she'd openly admitted that not two minutes ago!

My captor pressed a warm, gentle hand against the back of my waist. She guided me out into the darkness. We didn't meet anyone in the hall or on the stairs, but when we got down to the dark kitchen, Barry and his father were just coming inside through the back door. Barry was holding a small penlight, and the two of them were having a low, earnest conversation. At first they didn't even see us. Mopsy tried to move me back into the shadows, but before she could, my sky-high hair brushed against a hanging copper pot, clanking it into the one beside it.

Barry and his father stopped short and shone their little light at us. "Kate?" Barry said, sounding puzzled. "Mrs. Kingsley?"

Mopsy pressed her hand against my back, and I wondered if she'd managed to slip the gun down into her fingers. "Uh . . . hi, Barry," I said. Desperately I tried to think of some way of sending him a message without Mopsy figuring out what I was doing. This was probably going to be my only chance to escape. "We were just upstairs," I said brightly. "Trying to steal a look at the view from the balcony. Why, it's so clear, you could almost see *China* from up there! *Boy* I wish I could have had your telescope, Barry, like I did the other day." Pretty feeble, right? But please remember there was a gun in my back!

Barry frowned, started to say something, and then stopped and looked perplexed. His father put a hand on his shoulder. "Didn't Hettie ask you to go see about replacing that fuse, son?" he asked in a quiet voice. He turned toward Mopsy and me. "It seems there's some kind of problem with the lights in the house," he explained. "Waldo's too busy to fix it, so Barry's helping out. He knows his way around the cellar pretty well."

The Williams, father and son, turned to walk out of the room. My heart sank. But then Barry stopped, turned around again, and flashed his light at us. "Uh, Kate, would you . . . ?" All at once, he swept out his arm and gave Mopsy a violent push. CRACK! The blast of the shot sounded right next to my ear. Fortunately, though, since Mopsy was in the process of toppling over backward, the bullet didn't hit me, but shot straight upward and zinged into my old friend, the copper pot.

Everything started happening at once. Holding an

enormous torch flashlight, Brewster rushed into the room. Then Bonnie charged into the kitchen, closely followed by Waldo, Hettie, Marilyn, and Eunice. Finally Sergeant Schott came in with red-faced Theo at his side. For a few seconds everyone just stood and stared at one another in the eerie illumination from the torch. Then Mopsy got to her feet and stepped out into the spotlight.

"I'm so sorry to be the one to tell you this, Eunice dear," she announced, gesturing at me. "I discovered Bonnie's little friend here going through my jewels. I very much fear we'll have to have her arrested."

"You've *got* to be kidding!" I said. The woman really was unbelievable! But wait a minute. *Was* she so unbelievable? I mean, realistically speaking, who was Sergeant Schott more likely to take seriously? Kate Clancy, a fourteen-year-old California nobody, or Mopsy Kingsley, a kindly Boston society matron?

Fortunately it didn't come down to her word against mine. "Sorry, Mrs. Kingsley," Sergeant Schott said. "That story won't wash. Your husband has already told us all about your insurance fraud scheme."

"Oh, Theo, dear," Mopsy said softly. "Once again I'm afraid you've landed us in a sticky situation." As she spoke, Mopsy stared down toward the shadows on the floor behind where we were standing. At first I thought she was just embarrassed, but suddenly I realized what she was doing.

"The gun!" I yelled. As I shouted, I spotted the ugly little thing lying right next to the bottom step. With astonishing speed for such a portly person, Mopsy lunged for the floor. Fortunately I lunged a fraction of a second sooner, managing to snatch up the gun just before the older woman could grab it. Then I made a spectacular flying leap across the width of the kitchen, tossing the gun to Sergeant Schott as if it were a live python. It was the best broad jump I've ever made. If only I could perform that way in gym class!

Anyway, after that, Sergeant Schott took over as ringleader of the circus. A few more police officers arrived, and Mopsy and Theo were taken off in a police car. With her usual concern for others, Eunice remembered that there was still a party going on outside, and she and Brewster went outside to say good-bye to the guests and give them some idea of what was going on.

The rest of us started wandering into the living room and collapsing on chairs, couches, and cushions. I felt awful, and my reflection in a nearby china cabinet told me I looked just like I felt. Throughout all the excitement my Bride of Frankenstein makeup had held up only too well, and I still would have made the perfect match for the monster himself.

While I was still gazing at my reflection, Barry came in and flopped down on the cushion next to me. For a few seconds we stared at each other, as if neither one of us could believe what we'd just been through. Then Barry grinned his wise-guy grin. "You look radiant in that outfit," he said.

"Well you look like a bum in yours!" I shot back. We

both giggled at our own low-grade wit. Then I ordered myself to get serious. "Uh, actually, I guess I should be thanking you instead of making fun of you, Barry. I mean, I guess you sort of saved my life back there in the kitchen."

Barry's grin faded and his brown eyes got bigger than ever. "Do you really think Mopsy would have shot you?" he asked.

"I don't know," I said. "Through the whole thing she acted like her same sweet, vague self. But underneath all that she really seemed desperate—and obsessed with the idea of needing more money. Anyway it was a good thing you picked up on the clues I gave you."

"Clues? What clues?"

"You know! The stuff I said about seeing China and using a telescope and everything. I thought that's why you knocked Mopsy over!"

Barry looked puzzled. "Oh, that stuff," he said. "I couldn't figure out what in the world you were talking about. There I was, telling my father what a nice girl you were, and how we should go visit you in Los Angeles, and you show up babbling like you've drunk a whole bowlful of champagne punch!"

"Oh," I said in a small voice. "Oh. You thought I was drunk. So then why did you take it into your head to sock Mopsy?"

"Easy. I knocked her over because her sleeve fell sideways when I shone my light on her, and I saw a gun in her hand!"

Well when Barry said that, I felt as if I'd just swallowed a whole mixing bowl full of emotions. I was sick that I'd come so close to being abandoned in a criminal's clutches, annoyed that Barry hadn't caught onto my clever message, and relieved and grateful that he'd saved me anyway. Oh, yes. And I was embarrassed but happy that he'd been telling his father what a nice girl I was, particularly when I'd been thinking he hated me.

After having a taste of all those feelings, I finally decided to "Think Positive" and concentrate on relief, gratitude, and happiness. After all, I was alive, and the whole escapade was just about finished. All over but the shouting, as my grandma likes to say. And all over but the after-the-crime postmortem.

21

Actually it took a while for the after-the-crime postmortem to get going. Eunice and Brewster had to get rid of all the other guests, Hettie and Waldo had to put away the most perishable leftovers, and Sergeant Schott had to complete a lot of forms in triplicate at the police station. Finally, though, at sometime way past midnight, everybody was collected in the colossal living room. We were all droopy-eyed with exhaustion, but we were too worked up to sleep. And the questions were buzzing around the room like a bunch of maniacal mosquitoes.

"It just doesn't make sense to me," Hettie kept saying. "Why Theo Kingsley would want to steal his own wife's jewelry."

Sergeant Schott patiently explained that Theo hadn't really been stealing from Mopsy. "They were a team," he said. "She pretended to be upset when her things were taken, but in fact she was the one who was actually stealing her own stuff. We're still not sure if they sold the jewels or held onto them, but we're checking it out, and I'm sure we'll know soon."

"I can't imagine Mopsy giving up her family's heirlooms," Eunice said. "She treasured them so much." At that moment, as if on cue, a uniformed policewoman entered the room. She was holding a scraggly looking object in her hands. I recognized it in an instant. "My dead geranium!" I cried.

"We found a bracelet and a brooch buried in the bottom of the pot, Sergeant," the woman said. "Most of the dirt had been removed and replaced with the jewels."

Of course! I remembered the Kingsleys telling me they usually stayed in my room. They'd probably used the pot to stash their stolen pearls last summer and then decided it was such a good hiding place they might as well sneak in and hide this year's loot there as well until they had a chance to smuggle it out of the house. I silently predicted that the police would find Mopsy's missing pearl necklace somewhere in the Kingsleys' Boston house."

"What I don't understand," Eunice was asking, "is

why it was necessary for them to make me appear to be a kleptomaniac."

"As a cover," answered the sergeant. "A smokescreen. Originally they'd planned to fake a break-in from the outside, but apparently they got their wires crossed and everyone guessed the first burglary was an inside job. After that they made a new plan. Mopsy reasoned that if everyone thought Mrs. Bennington was responsible for little things disappearing and reappearing all over the house, no one would be likely to suspect an insurance scam on the part of the Kingsleys, and no one would come completely clean with the police. Also, from what I can figure Mrs. Kingsley has always been pretty jealous of Mrs. Bennington, and the jealousy has grown a lot more intense ever since the Kingsleys started having money problems. I think she may have gotten some enjoyment out of everyone thinking her elegant friend Eunice was wandering around the house taking things."

Eunice looked appalled, and Brewster looked irate, and it suddenly dawned on me that this whole thing must be even more ghastly for them than it had been for everybody else. To have your oldest and dearest friends turn out to be thieves who were using you as a cover-up for their own crimes . . . yuck. As I craned my neck to look at Eunice, I tried to imagine what reassuring thing she would have said to me if our situations were reversed. "Mopsy seemed to feel a desperate need for money," I said. "But she told me she hadn't really ever intended to hurt you."

Eunice reached over to squeeze my shoulder. "In a way I blame myself," she began. "We knew the Kingsleys had had some financial setbacks, and . . . perhaps if we'd offered to help . . ."

She was interrupted by Brewster's loud snort. "Really, my dear," he said, "that is absurd. If they were truly desperate, they could have come to us for a loan. But I know for a fact that their straits were not that dire. If Mopsy hadn't insisted on trying to live in the grand style of her girlhood, they would have had a perfectly adequate income."

At that point Barry and Marilyn's father spoke up for the first time. His quiet, soft-spoken voice reminded me of Marilyn's. "What I don't understand," he said, "is how the Kingsleys could have anticipated all the crazy things that would happen around here. First we have my two kids filching back the two china statuettes Theo must have taken from my shop. Then, from what I understand, we have *you*, sir," he paused and glanced at his father-in-law, "actually *returning* some of the things Theo and Mopsy had been stealing to use as plants for their kleptomania cover. How did the Kingsleys cope with that?"

"Well apparently you all did give them some problems with all your sneaking around," said Sergeant Schott. "How was anyone to believe Mrs. Bennington was a kleptomaniac when no one would admit anything was missing? As an example, we have the story Mr. Kingsley told us down at the station just now. Apparently, as you just guessed, Mr. Williams, Kingsley stole a china boy

143

and girl from your shop in the village. He planted them right out in the open in this room so everyone would think Mrs. Bennington had slipped them into her pocket and brought them back here. But by the next day the girl was back in the shop window. And as for the china boy, well, Theo says he had to steal it *again* when he discovered it in a bicycle carrying case in a cookie shop in Provincetown!"

Barry and I glanced at each other and then burst out in loud guffaws. Everyone looked at us as if we'd cracked under the strain of recent events—which maybe we *had*. Sergeant Schott gave us a stern stare and went on with his explanation. "Kingsley snitched the boy for a second time and replanted it in Mrs. Bennington's drawer, where he hoped someone would discover it."

"That part worked," I said. "I did discover it there."

"Precisely. You discovered it and you assumed Mrs. Bennington had taken it and put it there. Correct?"

"Well, not exactly," I began. But I stopped before I could get started. The history of my relationship with that china boy was way too complicated to explain. As I remembered all the different places I'd discovered it, I shot Barry a sideways glance and then quickly looked away. I didn't think the sergeant would appreciate another outburst of hysterical guffawing.

"Mrs. Bennington and I would have called in the police after the first jewel theft, you understand, Sergeant," Brewster was saying in his chairman-of-the-board way, "but, though we never believed it for a moment ourselves, the clues did seem to point to someone from inside the house. We were concerned that . . ."

"That the inefficient police force would arrest the wrong member of your household? Well I shouldn't admit it, but you may have a point there, Mr. Bennington. We might have made a mistake. Even with all the problems they had, the Kingsleys were clever at covering their tracks. For instance, the morning they staged the theft from the jewelry box in their room, Mopsy invited herself along to watch Bonnie and Marilyn play tennis so she would have an alibi for the time when the brooch was *supposed* to have been stolen. No one ever suspected her of taking her own brooch from herself earlier in the day."

There was a rumbling sound from the corner, and we all realized that Waldo was trying to say something. It sounded like, "Thought they was thieves all along."

For some reason this know-it-all comment freaked me right out. Without really thinking about what I was doing, I twisted myself and glared at the man. "What exactly is your problem anyway, Waldo? I mean, if you really knew they was . . . er, *were* . . . thieves all along, why didn't you say anything to anybody? And why did you go to all that trouble trying to scare *me* half to death?"

Waldo responded to my questions with a mixed medley of muttering and mumbling which my better self told me to interpret as an apology. Hettie provided a translation. "What Waldo means to say is that he's never really trusted anyone besides me and the Benningtons. And he's really sorry he tried to scare you so badly, you'd go home, Kate. You see, Waldo and I think of the Benningtons as our own family. And Waldo doesn't see quite straight where the family is concerned. He knew something strange was happening in the house. So he thought that if he could frighten outsiders away, nothing bad could be discovered about any of us."

Well he'd done a great job, I thought, remembering the scene with the scythe on the balcony. But I didn't say so out loud. I didn't want to stir up any more trouble, just when things were getting settled down. And besides, Eunice and Brewster were both beaming gratefully at Waldo and Hettie, as if it didn't matter if the servants pitched the next set of visitors right into the ocean. So I made like a clam and didn't say anything more about it.

Marilyn asked what would happen to Theo and Mopsy next, and Sergeant Schott said they'd probably stand trial for theft and insurance fraud and possibly attempted assault against yours truly. He thought the police had a pretty good case against them, particularly now that some of the jewels had been recovered. Then he told everybody that he and the insurance investigators would probably be back in the morning, but that for now he was calling it a night. Everybody agreed that that was a good idea since it was now almost 2:00 A.M., but when the sergeant left, nobody made a move to go upstairs. Finally Hettie suggested whipping up something to eat, and I thought that was such a good idea, I decided to grant her husband a full pardon.

For quite a while after that everybody moved into the kitchen and munched on leftovers and talked. We were all in a sort of hyper-but-happy mood, and it made me realize how badly all the murky mysterious undercurrents had been dragging everyone down before. I mean, people were transformed. Gary, Barry's and Marilyn's dad, was chatting and laughing with Eunice and Brewster like there'd never been any problem between them at all. Bonnie and Marilyn were giggling over their paté sandwiches in the corner. And Hettie and Waldo were sitting at the kitchen table holding hands!

It was like being at a whole new party. Only one shocking thing happened. The hall clock struck BONG, BONG, BONG! three times, and in the same instant, the back door flew open. We all gasped out loud, expecting to see Mopsy float in and take us all hostage again or something. But then Great-Uncle Horace teetered in! Apparently he'd fallen asleep in the gazebo and when he'd woken up, the party had vanished. We invited him in, offered him a chair, and handed him an eclair. Within thirty seconds he was lecturing Bonnie and Marilyn about the leaves on the distant branches of the Bennington family tree. I exchanged one quick sympathetic look with Bonnie, just before her eyes glazed over.

After that Barry and I picked up right where we'd left off—munching on cold shrimp and planning what we'd do when his family came out to Los Angeles to visit. He'd already been to Disneyland, of course, but I told him about Knotts Berry Farm and Magic Mountain and eating homemade potato chips on the Santa Monica Pier and visiting Bruce the mechanical shark and going roller skating by the beach in Venice. I even got him excited about going to see the LaBrea Tar Pits! It was a great conversation.

The rest of my visit to Bluff Point Dunes was great too. The weather was gorgeous, so naturally we spent a lot of time at our own personal beach. But we also took some more bike trips, and went to see the sunrise over the bay, and found a pet turtle (named Myrtle, of course) in the woods by a pretty little pond just up the road from the cottage. We went to a clambake with some of Barry and Marilyn's friends from the village, and we even went back to Provincetown and revisited the cookie shop— twice. Marilyn came to sleep over one night, and she and Bonnie and I stayed up talking for hours. By the end of the two weeks, I felt as if I had two new lifelong best friends.

But anyway, as my corny old dad always says when he's scraping the last spoonful of Häagen-Dazs out of the carton, all good things must come to an end. When our final morning came around, I felt sort of mixed-up. On the one hand, the two weeks had gone incredibly fast, and I couldn't believe it was already over. On the other hand, so many astonishing things had happened, I felt like I'd lived there for an eternity.

After our final breakfast Hettie and Waldo came out of the kitchen to say good-bye. For the very first time Waldo gave me my very own personalized scrunched-up smile, and I was so pleased, I knew I really had forgiven him. Hettie went one step further and actually took hold of my hand. "Please come back with Bonnie again next summer, Kate," she said. "And stay for longer than just two weeks." What a good idea, I thought.

The Benningtons were driving us back to the Boston airport, so we didn't have to say good-bye to them for a while, but we did have to say good-bye to Barry and Marilyn and their father. This wasn't easy, because as you may have noticed, I like Marilyn, and I *really* like Barry. Still it wasn't as hard as I'd thought it would be, because Barry's father announced that their family would definitely be coming out to L.A. at the end of the summer.

"I'll hire you as my tour guide, Kate," Barry said when we had a few seconds alone. "Your salary will be all the chocolate chip cookies you can eat. Okay?"

"Sure," I said. That same old witty response. I promised myself that by August I'd think of something more original to say.

We scribbled down our addresses and phone numbers, and then it was time to go. We stuffed all our things into the old Mercedes, and then Brewster climbed behind the wheel, started the car, and smashed the accelerator all the way to the floor. As we barreled down the driveway in a cloud of dust, I swiveled my head around and stared back at the outline of Bluff Point Dunes Cottage against the bright blue sky. I didn't stop staring until the very last peak of the pointed roof had vanished from my sight. Then I reluctantly turned forward again, and immediately

149

gouged my nails into my palms as Brewster sashayed the car back and forth along the road.

I'll spare you the details of the trip back to Boston, except to say that we got there alive, and that the nervous twitch in my eye went away almost immediately after we climbed out of the car. Inside the airport Eunice and Brewster hugged and kissed me good-bye as if they were my very own grandmama and grandpapa, which I almost wished they could be. (Not really, Grandma Irene and Grandpa Mike. I'll always love you best.) They hugged and kissed Bonnie, too, of course, and then we said good-bye and went through the entrance and boarded the plane.

A few minutes later, as we sped down the runway and lifted up into the sky over Massachusetts, I pressed my face against the window and stared out at a fluffy cloud. What a fantastic place, I thought. What an experience. Once again, shy, neurotic, anxiety-ridden Kate Clancy had drawn upon some unknown inner resources, solved a mystery, and survived an exciting adventure. It was a real once-in-a-lifetime episode. Even if I never got to visit there again in my whole life, I'd never ever forget my visit to Bluff Point Dunes.

Get ready to go back to your ho-hum existence, Clancy, I told myself. You'll never have another such mysterious, intriguing, scary, romantic escapade.

Ha! myself answered. *Don't be too sure about that!*

Which one of my selves is right? I don't have a clue. But I promise you this. If anything this interesting ever happens to me again, I'll let you know about it.

ABOUT THE AUTHOR

Lisa Eisenberg was born in Flushing, New York, and grew up in the Midwest. She received her B.A. from Swarthmore College in Swarthmore, Pennsylvania, and worked as an editor for several publishing companies before collaborating with Katy Hall on several joke books, *Fishy Riddles*, *Buggy Riddles*, and the forthcoming *Grizzly Riddles*, for Dial. Her first novel, *Mystery at Snowshoe Mountain Lodge*, also published by Dial, introduced junior sleuth Kate Clancy and her friends. Ms. Eisenberg lives with her husband and two children in Ithaca, New York.